the christmas war paws

An Enemies to Lovers, Second Chance Christmas Romance Novella

terreece m clarke

lifeslice media

Copyright © 2023 by Terreece M. Clarke

All rights reserved.

Published by LifeSlice Media

No part of this book may be reproduced in any form or by any electronic or mechanical means, including information storage and retrieval systems, without written permission from the author, except for the use of brief quotations in a book review.

This is a work of fiction. Any similarity between the characters and situations within its pages and places or persons, living or dead, is unintentional and co-incidental.

author's note

TW/CW things to note - 'open door adult intimacy,' light exhibitionism, death of a parent, swearing.

Also, there are dialect and grammar choices that are intentional and specific to the regions and cultures highlighted.

If you believe you've found an editing error, first yell your favorite expletive, then shoot the team an email where I too will yell my favorite expletive - hint it begins with an f. Then I shall fix it while raging. It's cathartic. [sbrent@lifeslicemedia.com]

The Christmas War Paws Playlist
Apple Music: https://apple.co/3tqxgYW
Spotify: https://spoti.fi/3TxOw9u

praise for terreece m clarke

The Courageous Love Series

"A beautifully written story full of heart, suspense, and love."

— J. L. Seegars, author of Restore Me

"To say this sweeping story is amazing would be an understatement."

— CLorraine Kibler, GoodReads.com

I was NOT ready 💟💟 This book [was] everything, gave what it was supposed to have given, left nothing on the table, it was full full after it ate.

— Chriss Mountain, GoodReads.com

It is so rare to find a new author that can "hit it out of the park" on their first go, but Ms. Clarke has done it.

— GDotz, Amazon.com Review

Dedicated to those who wish holiday movies had a little more spice. And swearing. And puppies.

the christmas war paws playlist

1. freeze
1. I'll Be Home for Christmas | PJ Morton

2. take off your pants
1. Savage Remix | Meg the Stallion featuring Beyonce

3. on sight
1. This Christmas | Donny Hathaway

4. 'paws'
1. Blue Christmas | Aretha Franklin

5. bearded gingerbread men
1. Whistle (While You Work It) | Katy Tiz
2. Run This Town | Jay-Z and Rihanna

6. mr. right now
1. Let It Snow | Boyz II Men

7. unleashed

1. Hurt You | Toni Braxton + Babyface

8. hate you

1. Eye Hate U | Prince

9. one to go

1. Feenin' | Jodeci

10. always time for pie

1. Who Would Have Though | Boyz II Men

11. hit out

1. My Heart is Calling | Whitney Houston

12. grand gesture

1. I Believe in You and Me | Whitney Houston
2. Move Bitch | Ludacris

13. you have me

1. Silent Night | The Temptations

1
freeze

francesca

"WHAT THE HELL?!"

One minute I'm opening the door to my grandmother's house, the next, a furry blur streaks past my ankles and slips through the posts of the porch railing. Turning too quickly, I caught sight of a scruffy Staffordshire Bull Terrier puppy right before I slipped backwards off the side of the back steps.

As I stared at the clear winter sky, waiting for my breathing to return to normal, the endless stars twinkled merrily back at me.[1] It took a moment for me to realize what happened, but before I could worry too much about the deep pain in my ribs and right ankle, a tortured little whimper distracted me. I rolled over with a grunt. The throbbing parts of me and the wet snow that seeped through my jeans, down my boots and deeeep into the neck of my sweater became unimportant as I crawled to the shivering, four-legged soul trapped under the rotted remains of the step railing.

"I'm coming, doggo," I whispered, hoping to soothe it and motivate myself to close the gap between it and me. It was so cold my face was already numb. The rest of my body was joining it, except my knee, where a sticky, wet warmth spread. I was bleeding and annoyed.

Seriously, who skins their knee at my age?

Gingerly, I pulled the rotted wood away from the dog until I got to the last piece and noticed a good amount of blood that didn't belong to me.

"Shit puddin'. You've got a nail stuck directly in your little leg."

I snatched off my giant scarf and wrapped it firmly around its leg where the small piece of wood was still painfully attached. I swept the rest of the scarf around its wet, shivering body.

After finding my bag, I kept one hand on the pup and stretched for my giant purse. He whimpered, and I yelped as my ribs protested any movement that involved stretching. After I scooped the dog into my bag, I gently lifted his head out and he gifted me with a lovely little lick across my exposed wrist.

"Don't thank me just yet. We still need to get you to a vet. The good news is we can get anywhere in this town in seven minutes. The bad news is everything in this place shuts down by eight… and it's close to midnight."

I was a sweaty, shivery, soaking pile of aches when I finally got myself and the dog in my giant purse out of the yard, safely loaded in the car and to the only vet in town. The pup's breath grew more rapid as I banged on the door of the house beside the vet clinic where old Mr. Bing, the local vet, and his family, lived. I checked the pup's gums and noted they were pale - not good.

"Think, think, think..." Taking a chance, I limp-hopped to the door of the clinic and tried it. Unlocked.

"Good old Ohio Falls where no one locks their doors at night, even with thousands of dollars of equipment and medications for the taking." Shaking my head at the naivete, I hop-limped fully into the clinic, past the waiting room, and into the treatment area, flipping lights on as I went.

I placed the pup carefully on the examination table and took a moment to soothe his restlessness. No doubt he'd either been to a vet before or the smell of other animals in the room made him anxious.

"It's okay Puddin.' Let's get you —"

"FREEZE!" a gruff voice growled into the room. "Whatever drugs you're looking for, we don't have them."

I froze, head-to-head with Puddin.' He kept his baleful eyes on me as he froze, too. It would have been funny if I wasn't worried there was gun pointed at my back.

"I'm Dr. Francesca Johnson-DeWitt. I'm visiting to arrange my grandmother's affairs but had a run in with this little guy. I'm a licensed veterinarian, both here in Ohio and California. I banged on Mr. Bing's door for help. I didn't realize he was no longer practicing, and not to scold, but if you don't want people waltzing in looking for drugs, lock the door."

"Frankie? Frankie Johnson?" a feminine voice called out.

"It's Francesca. No one ever calls me Frankie but, wait, Tonya Bing is that you?"

"Yes! Girl, come give me a hug!"

"I would, but I've got a gun pointed at me and I'd like to keep what brains I have left inside my skull."

"Oh, Sebastian just has a bat," Tonya laughed merrily.

Taking my forehead off Puddin's I turned slowly, partly out of caution, partly out of the pounding pain radiating through my body and partly because the very last person I wanted to see was the adult version of the idiot who took my virginity at twenty, exploited me, and forced me into exile.

I took a deep, painful breath and stood squarely on shaky legs. Sure enough, standing shirtless in the doorway wearing low slung basketball shorts, armed with a metal bat, was Sebastian "Fuck Face" Bing.

"Fuck Face. I see you're still threatening women."

"Ditzy DeWitt. I see you're still single-handedly decreasing the collective IQ of the surrounding area."

2
take off your pants

francesca

"NOT THIS AGAIN," Tonya muttered as she peered over the top of her brother's shoulder into the examination room. "Move Sebbie."

Moving Sebastian aside, she waddled into the room, her pregnant belly leading the way. "Frankie, you may not be an addict, but you have to be high as Cootie Brown. Why do you have a wet dog bleeding into a Birkin bag?"

"It's just an overnight bag," I muttered, as I turned my face from Sebastian's twisted one, and willed all the old embarrassment away. My focus was on Puddin'.

"I've started his assessment, and he's showing signs of shock. He may need a transfusion. Where's your dad? We should start typing his blood and bring in a donor dog. Help me get him started on fluids, and if you know where he keeps the keys to the med cabinet, I can get him a little more comfortable with his pain before we remove this nail and—"

"What in the hell do you think you're doing?" Sebastian

asked. "There's no way in hell I'm letting you practice hopscotch in my clinic, let alone medicine. I don't need another Ditzy DeWitt Lawsuit ruining my life."

"Ruining YOUR life?! I—"

"Doctors! Cool it. Frankie, our dad retired. *We* run the practice now, and I'd love for you to assist girl, though... Well, honey, you look like you fell off a roof."

"Nope, just over the side of Grandma Mabel's back steps."

"Oh my God! Sebbie, go check her over. She's limping."

"Tonya, I'm fine. Just need a little ibuprofen and some dry clothes." I waved Sebastian away like he was a fruit fly trying to dive bomb a sweet drink.

"Scrubs are in the cabinet over there. You can change in the next room, but I'm not letting you back in *this* room until you get checked out."

Puddin' whimpered from the table, his eyes on her.

"Don't worry Puddin', she's bluffing," I whispered, as I tried my best to walk normally to the cabinet.

"I am not. Sebbie, help her out," Tonya bossed in the way only a little sister can.

"Fine," he growled.

Sebastian swooped me up, bridal style, which was a completely unnecessary display of strength.

"Ew, put me down. I have no desire to be this close to your man nipples." I threw in a few fake retches to make myself sound more convincing and to stop my brain from rolling back to freshman year of college where I very much desired to be close to his man nipples.

I held myself stiff as he silently strode to the adjacent room. I tried not to notice his still very nice body, broader and more filled out, or his bare feet or the way he smelled - cinnamon and soap.

Nope.

I hated this man. Solidly. I just... It had been a long time since I've been in a man's arms. Two and a half years. Two years, six months, twelve days - and if my internal clock was correct - thirteen, fourteen, fifteen seconds.

God, how I hate my husband. And Sebastian Bing. And men in general. I am just too heterosexual. Maybe I haven't met the right girl...

"I remember a time when you couldn't get enough of my nipples," Fuck Face said, interrupting my thoughts. "That and Cask and Cream."

"Now I am really going to be sick. Put me down Fuck Face."

"Whatever," he groused and set me, with surprising softness, near a human exam table before he took a step back, crossed his arms and glared at me. "Take off your pants."

"What? Forget it. I'll sit in the waiting room." I started my hop-limp journey when he grabbed me and picked me up near my waist and oof, the pain... It radiated from the moment he touched me, wrapping around my lungs like a vise. My back stiffened, my jaw locked, and it was so intense I saw stars.

sebastian

All thoughts - like how much I still desperately hated her and how she was the same selfish brat who didn't care about the things people worked their whole lives for, like an expensive designer purse, and the thoughts on how soft she was in my arms, and how she still smelled the same - flew out of my mind the moment she seized up.

Before she could protest, I lifted her heavy, wet sweater to the side to assess her injuries. Bruises formed along her lower ribs on the right side of her body, marring the soft skin down to her hip.

"You're going to need X-rays. Do you remember if you lost consciousness when you fell?"

She sucked in a wince when I manipulated the area.

"I just got the wind knocked out of me," she said through gritted teeth. "I'm afraid Puddin' got the worst of it. He ended up underneath the railing somehow."

"Outside of me, Tonya's the best. He's in excellent hands."

I don't know why I wanted to assuage the She Beast's worry, but I did. "I'm going to need you to get undressed so I can check you over. Can you get out of these wet clothes?"

"Tonya's always been smarter than the both of us... And of the three of us, you've always been several points behind," she smirked. She tried to lift her sweater over her head and failed.

"No more than two points and you know it. *And* I was getting my MD and DVM simultaneously," I reminded her as I helped ease her arm out of the sleeve, noting the wood debris caught in her sister locs and running down her back.

"Same argument, same rebuttal. Nothing's changed."

She gave me a genuine smile and suddenly I saw her like she had been all those years ago. As suddenly as her smile came, it left when she seemed to remember who we were now.

After I cleared my throat to get past the sudden tightness in my chest, my voice came out harsher than I intended.

"Everything's changed, DeWitt. No need to go down memory lane."

She looked away from me and took a deep breath.

I cleared my throat again and focused on removing her boots.

"Are your feet always this swollen?" I checked the right against the left, noticing the asymmetry.

"I'm on new blood pressure medications. My doc said it should resolve itself as I adjust to them."

"Which ones?" I grabbed a clipboard and started making notes.

She rattled off the medications and dosages.

She's awfully young for that combination... "Why—"

"My heart doesn't relax. Initially, the first medication worked well at lowering my systolic, but my diastolic stubbornly refused to cooperate. It's stress," she shrugged and looked at her hands.

"Mm..."

"Look, let's not pretend you give a damn. I probably have a sprained ankle and slightly bruised ribs. Nothing a few weeks on the beaches of the Bahamas can't cure. Take your X-rays and let me get dressed to assist."

"Fine." I stood back and watched her struggle on one foot to get impossibly tight, wet jeans off. "Any year now DeWitt."

"I jump to put on jeans. You're going to have to give me a minute," she huffed in frustration and obvious pain.

9

"Oh, for the love of —," I swiped a pair of trauma shears, bent in front of her and cut her jeans off, starting at the ankle. I had to grip her waistband tightly as I worked. "Stop wiggling DeWitt, the sooner I get these off, the sooner you can get the hell out of my clinic and life."

"You unprofessional, arrogant—"

"And you're a spoiled, recalcitrant She Beast..." I barked back, snipping the last of her jeans on one side. As I started on the right leg, she swore up a storm. I ignored her, swiftly shearing the fabric from her body. As I peeled it away from her right knee, she hissed again.

"Sorry... you've got an abrasion here... just let me..."

She stood still as I worked the material away from the clotted wound. After I removed the material, she sat back on the exam table so I could clean her up, do the x-rays and wrap her ankle. Once I finished everything and was satisfied that she didn't need further care, I knelt low to the floor with a pair of scrub pants.

"Hold on to me and step into them."

"Oh, get off!" Instead of following my directions, she attempted to dress herself. On one foot. Like some wet, shivering, injured, asshole flamingo. Trying to keep my irritation at bay, I attempted to help her ass, again. "Don't be dumb DeWitt, just let me help you."

She shoved me away, and I fell backward. I still held the scrubs tight in my hand which cause her to tip forward toward me.

CRASH!

Supplies clanged around me, a hard knee dug into my diaphragm and barely there satin panties tickled my nose.

"Do you mind getting your vagina out of my face?"

With a yelp she rolled off me, but not before her knee dug in a little further. *Heffa.*

"My vagina was not in your face, and I think a medical professional would know that."

"I'm adding assault to your breaking and entering charges."

"And I'm shaking in my boots," she quipped as she hopped into the bottoms and out the door.

"It is a pleasure to work with you again, Dr. Frankie," Tonya said as DeWitt finished the last of the sutures.

Smiling at her, Francesca winked. "Thank you for throwing me a bone. I felt like I needed to be the one to take care of him. I don't know how long he was on Grandma Mabel's porch all by himself. Was he chipped?"

"No, and he's never been here before. I'd recognize such a handsome boy anywhere."

"Can I stay with him tonight?"

"Yes."

"No."

"Sebbie."

Rolling my eyes, I threw up a hand. "Whatever. Nothing she can steal anyway."

"Do you wake up being an asshole, or does it take practice?"

"You just bring it out of me naturally, DeWitt. Tonya, I'll set up the overnight room. Get off your feet."

Tonya saluted me with a grin. Ignoring DeWitt, I went back to the house and got the nice sheets instead of the normal ones we used for patients. Tonya would likely have told me to do it, anyway. I just hope the She Beast doesn't swipe them.

Tonya - I made French toast for you and baby. Yes, that kind. You are out of vanilla. I'll be back for Puddin' after I see Grandma Mabel's lawyer.

Fuck Face - None for you. Suck it.

-Francesca

"Ooooh she made banana Japanese French Toast! I haven't had this since college!"[1]

My sister, a mere eighteen months younger, a woman who I've known my whole life, my business partner, sat down to a plate of banana Japanese French Toast without sending as much as a glance my way.

"Come on Sissy, let me get a piece."

Cough. Cough. Cough.

"Did you just *cough* on your plate? What are you, five?"

"Nope, I'm pregnant and starving. Maybe you should try talking to Frankie instead of regressing. This beef? It's gone on too long."

I glanced out the window after noticing a growing number of neighbors gathering in front of the house. Moving closer, I saw what the neighbors were gawking at -

my inflatable Christmas decorations were in some very inappropriate positions.

DeWitt. Next time I see her? It's on sight.

Clearing my throat, I opened the front door.

"Mayor Garrett, it was a vandal. She's about five feet, five..."

3
on sight

francesca

I WATCHED Sebastian play with the kids in the middle of the town square.[1]

In the summer, the green space was full of families playing frisbee, picnicking and having a great time. The winter was no less festive. Instead of children throwing frisbees there was a small group of kids having a snowball fight behind little hills of snow. Their squeals of delight lent a jovial atmosphere to families and tourists taking in the holiday decorations. Already irritated that Grandma Mabel's lawyer missed our meeting, I grew more annoyed as I watched Sebastian. His smug, stupid smile beamed as he played with the kids.

The surrounding women were swooning. I mean, he was a tall, thick, handsome, dual degreed doctor with pretty teeth, waves so deep you'd get seasick... And bearded? Sure, he looked great, wholesome, even, especially in that sappy holiday sweater, but I knew who he really was.

SPLAT!

As I wiped snow out of my eyes, I smiled, ready to reassure whichever kid that accidentally got me. That was until my sight cleared and I saw Fuck Face grinning as he casually tossed around a second snowball.

"On Sight," he mouthed.

My right side was still sore, so my return throw was trash. It didn't make it halfway to him. The bastard whizzed a second one at me. I dodged that one, but the movement left me unsteady on my damn ankle. Sebastian had the good sense to look slightly remorseful.

"You want me to hit him for you?" a voice piped up.

I looked down into the eager eyes of the cutest little hero. He had to be about nine or ten. Never one to waste an opportunity...

"What's your name?"

"JD ma'am."

"Nice to meet you JD, I'm Ms. Francesca and yes. I want you to hit him with as many snowballs as you can. I wish you could hit him with 1000 snowballs and get your friends to hit him with 1000 snowballs. I wish you would bury him in snowballs as high as he is tall and as wide as he is muscled."

The kid's eyes grew in excitement and a bit of alarm. I sounded crazy, but that man brought out the vicious competitor in me. I worked my ass off to beat him in every test in college and clinched the most coveted internship for our veterinarian program. He made me crazy.

Francesca you cannot enlist kids to throw snowballs at adults!

But it was too late. Before I could get my brain to come back from the dark side, the first snowball landed right smack in the middle of his smug, stupid, objectively handsome face. Heaven help me, I had not laughed that hard in months, years even. It was gold - cold, slippery mess sliding down that surprised, stupid face.

"Good job kid, that was perfect, but you shouldn't hit him again."

"I'll hit him 1000 times just for you."

OK well now I feel a little guilty.

Obviously, the young guy was smitten with me. But after two globs hit me in rapid succession, Sebastian had sealed his own fate. I'm not proud of it, but I nodded, smiled, and threw my arm out Vanna White-style, giving full permission for destruction.

Twenty minutes later, the merry families fled and, in their place, reinforcements poured in from all corners of the town in the form of the football and baseball teams of Ohio Falls Middle School and practically every girl from Ohio Falls Middle School. You'd think the girls would have sided with me, the actual victim, but nooo... they stood on the side of the hunky vet who helps puppies. Booo...

At this point, mounds of snow forts covered the square. Organized teams used assembly lines to create snowballs, throwers and infantry were tasked with taking over positionally superior forts. It was organized-ish chaos. From my perch on my snow chair—the creativity of kids, I tell ya—I tried to keep my troops in line, but when you have an entire middle school at war, there's bound to be a couple of people who catch strays.

Like the mayor of Ohio Falls.

Time slowed as an adorable little girl, doing the absolute most in an all pink, fuzzy ensemble, sent a beautifully arched snowball toward my lieutenant whose uncle drove one of the city's snowplows. JD waved triumphantly, and the snowplow followed, bringing in fresh artillery. Then JD crossed paths with the Mayor. I know he was the mayor because he had a little ribbon on his thick shearling jacket that said "Mayor." In a town of 15,000, I'm not quite sure why he needed to identify himself, but there you go. And so did his hat. Go, that is.

"He started it."

"She started it with my inflatables."

"Destruction of property. Blockading of city streets without a permit. Misuse of city equipment. Assault on a government official." The mayor, with slow deliberate movements, leaned down and picked up his hat. Shaking the snow off, he put the skully back on. "Who are you, ma'am, so I know whose name to list on the arrest warrant?"

I sighed, shifted, and glared at Sebastian, who stood there with a stupid, sloppy grin on his face.

I should smack that dumb grin right off.

"Did you just say you wanted to smack our veterinarian?"

"I didn't mean to say out loud. I'm Francesca Johnson-DeWitt, Dr. Francesca Johnson-DeWitt and I'm here to—"

"You're Mabel's granddaughter? Oh Francesca! We are so glad to have you back." He reached out and hugged me.

My eyebrows shot to the sky.

"I'm Dominic Garrett and I am so sorry to hear about your grandmother."

I felt my face drop and that pain that has lived in my chest for decades grew more acute. I couldn't quite meet his eyes when I thanked him.

"Your grandmother was an integral part of this town and boy, was she proud of you."

My head lifted in surprise.

"Me?"

"Yes, your grandmother talked about you all the time, telling everyone all that you were doing, about your practice, and how it was thriving."

Embarrassed, I didn't want to admit I had no idea what he was talking about. If what he said was true, I wondered why she never bothered to say anything to me before she died. Instead, I plastered a benign smile on my face, nodded and waited.

"Listen," he smiled, taking my arm. "Let's forget all about this—"

"Wait you're just going to let her go after all the trouble she caused?" Sebastian protested.

"All the trouble I caused? I've got a bad ankle and bruised ribs! What harm could I have possibly caused?"

"You have a barely twisted ankle and a couple boo boos."

"Right... Francesca, you should join us at our town hall meeting this Saturday. We're going over *Deck the Holiday Week* activities. Maybe you can stand in for your grandmother as restitution for this overzealous winter fun. Mabel made sure that the Christmas holiday went off without a hitch every year. I bet you inherited some of those organizational skills and obviously you have a way with people." He nodded toward the kids collecting discarded mittens, shovels, and other war paraphernalia.

"Oh, I don't think—"

"That wasn't a suggestion."

"Ah."

"I'll see you too Sebastian. You messed around and finally gave me a reason to loop you in. Thanks Francesca." Adjusting his hat, Mayor Garrett rambled confidently down the street. "I have the perfect project for you two to collaborate on."

"Shit. I hate you DeWitt."

"Hate you more Fuck Face."

4
'paws'

sebastian

"SHE'LL BE HERE," Tonya said as I glanced at the door.

"Who?"

"Frankie. You've been looking for her for the last fifteen minutes."

"I haven't been looking for anyone. I just wanted to see who was all coming. The crowd looks a little sparse tonight."

There were the usual suspects - the people who had to be there because they held some official role, the people who couldn't help themselves because they loved being involved in everyone's business, and a few people who actually had business. The meeting right before *Deck the Holiday Week* usually made for a packed house. The auditorium of City Hall held several hundred people, easily, but tonight most of the neatly ordered chairs sat empty, facing a long table where the mayor, secretary and other town dignitaries sat.

"Things haven't been the same since the last of the shipping hubs closed down, and now, with Miss Mabel gone, it doesn't really feel like Christmas, you know?"

"Yeah. But like Dad says, 'We'll make do with what we got.'"

Tonya smiled and pushed a hand against her lower rib. "I can't wait until he gets back. I also can't wait until this kid moves their foot out of my ribs." Suddenly, her eyes lit up, and she waved her hand. "Frankie, over here!"

DeWitt's eyes looked hesitant until they landed on me, then they iced over. Typical. She strolled toward us with Puddin' recuperating in her giant purse. Her footsteps echoed with an uneven gait across the wooden floor. She still favored her left ankle.

"Mr. Burnside, it's imperative we meet to complete my grandmother's affairs. This is the second time I've contacted you since you asked to reschedule. I have an upcoming trip and will out the country for some time. Please contact me by end of day tomorrow." Rolling her eyes as she clicked off the call, she sat and hugged Tonya tight.

"Hey girl." Her decidedly not a purse dog scrambled to get onto Tonya's lap. Settling gingerly against the two of them, its head rested against Tonya's stomach. DeWitt ignored me.

The mayor called the meeting to order and the secretary, Mrs. Shaw, recounted prior meeting minutes. Finally, after discussions on previous budget amendments, talk turned to *Deck the Holiday Week* business.

"Wait before we get to holiday week," Ms. Gladys interrupted. "I just want to know who's gonna clean up the town square? It's iced over in many parts now and if we're going to invite visitors here, we can't have riffraff running about and ruining my town's image."

"Not the riffraff." DeWitt said with a slight attitude.

"Just because *certain* people are related to the 'dearly departed'," she continued, "there are matriarchs that remain and want to keep the town held to a certain esteem. No disrespect to the dead, of course."

"Oh, that felt real disrespectful," Francesca muttered under her breath.

"This is not the first incident, and who knows how far it's going to go?" Gladys looked around with a sniff. "This unseemly Christmas war between Dr. Sebastian and *Mrs.* DeWitt is bad for business, bad for the town. The pornographic Christmas inflatables, the riot involving *children*... it's low class. There must be some accountability."

Francesca turned in her seat with a single raised brow and Puddin' popped his head up, joining her with a low growl. Before she could say a word, I was talking.

"DOCTOR Johnson-DeWitt. It's Doctor Johnson-DeWitt, Ms. Gladys, and you will address her as such. She has earned it and as a welcomed, *grieving* guest of Ohio Falls, I expect her to be treated with the kindness, respect, and hospitality we are known for."

I could feel everyone's eyes on me as I defended Francesca, but I didn't care. I eyeballed Ms. Gladys until she tersely nodded her agreement. Turning back toward the front of the room, I ignored Francesca's eyes burning a hole in the side of my face.

Mayor Garrett cleared his throat and raised his hands. "Let's get back to the matter at hand. Dr. Johnson-DeWitt and Dr. Bing have graciously agreed to help with *Deck the Holiday Week* as restitution—"

"We did?" We asked in unison.

One look from the Mayor and I heard Francesca sigh next to me.

"We did," she mumbled.

"—And they will channel their competitive energy into the traditional Holiday Week competitions *only*. While they will be the major draw, *everyone* has a chance to win each event. This pause in personal pranks will be permanent." He leveled a pointed gaze at us like we were teenagers.

"I say we go back to traditional Christmas events without input from outsiders," Ms. Gladys called out.

"Let me ask you, Dr. Johnson-DeWitt, as a visitor, what would bring you back to Ohio Falls at Christmas?"

Francesca looked around at all the eyes on her then focused on a space ahead of her, as she absentmindedly stroked Puddin'. Smiling, she seemed to pull up a happy memory.

"Well, I haven't been here since college, and even then, it was just on break, but Christmastime here was one of the most magical experiences I've ever had. When I think of the best Christmases ever, I think of this place. I'll do what I can to help, but I don't think anyone gives a fig about this loser and our personal issues."

Chuckles rumbled through the room before Bill, who owned a tow truck and hauling business, called out, "This is the most fun that the town has had in years. Sure, it's always great around Christmas, but your seasonal shenanigans have me glued to the town's social media pages. It's nice to see something other than bad news posted."

"We're on the town social media page?" Francesca whisper-asked Tonya.

"I agree, this Christmas War 'Paws,'" Tonya said as she

waved Puddin's paw in the air, "is going to be great for the town. These two have fired up the group chat. Our social media stats are climbing and bookings at the inn *and* hotel are filling up. If people see you two taking part, they'll want to participate or at least attend the events just to see what you get up to."

"There's a group chat? What group chat?" Francesca asked, this time with a bit of panic creeping into her voice.

"Then it's decided. The Bing / Johnson-DeWitt Christmas War is *PAWSed* for eternity and *Deck the Holiday Week* will feature these two competitors. The prize? Bragging rights and first song choice at the *Holiday Sprinkle Dance*."

"What's a holiday sprinkle dance? Sounds like a very specific kink," Francesca asked, befuddled. "Seriously, what just happened?"

Catching her eyes for the first time all night, I noticed they were lit by the nearby Christmas tree lights giving them a special glow. *Ugh.*

"What happened is you went to an Ohio Falls town meeting and got hustled."

francesca

As I walked out of the meeting into the crisp night air, the cloud covered sky highlighted the stillness of the night. The voices of meeting attendees trailed off as I strolled up the sidewalk toward home. [1]

What the hell have I gotten myself into? I am supposed to

be on an island drinking fruity drinks in a bikini. Yet here I am, freezing my behind off in Ohio Falls, going through my dead grandmother's stuff, engaged in some great holiday war.

"Small towns are a menace."

"Is that why you have you haven't been back?" Sebastian asked from beside me. I started, then stepped further over on the sidewalk. No reason to walk that close.

"Let's just say this town isn't for me."

"Oh really?" His dark brows raised as he mocked her. "I'm not surprised someone of your background looks down their nose at Ohio Falls.

"I'm not looking down my nose at anything. What I said back there was true. It's a great town. Just not for me and there's nothing wrong with that. You know what? I don't need to explain myself to you." I stepped up the pace to distance us.

"No, you don't have to explain yourself to anyone. You never have."

"And what's that supposed to mean, Sebastian?"

"It means I don't want you here. I've made a good life here and every time I see you, I'm reminded of everything that happened."

"OK, Fuck Face, what's your solution? Because I'm all ears. I'd rather not be a fugitive from small town justice."

"Easy. Our own side bet - I win, you leave Ohio Falls and never come back."

"Not a problem. I have no intention of coming back. And, if I win, you admit it. You man up after all these years and admit what you did."

His head jerked back in surprise and his face became a thundercloud. He was furious. The sharp, dark slash of his eyebrows dipped low.

"You mean to tell me, after all these years, you're still on that?"

I stopped mid-stride, stunned by his audacity. "Yes, Sebastian, I'm still on the fact that you are a liar, a thief, and an asshole. Was I supposed to get over that?!"

"You were supposed to realize I had nothing to do with it. That *you* made a monumental error and ruined my life!"

"You turned mine upside down and stole more from me than you realize. I won't just let that go."

"Well, your family didn't let it go for years, so like father, like daughter..."

"What are you talking about?!"

"What the hell ever, DeWitt."

"You guys!" Tonya fussed as she stepped between us, forcing us several paces apart to allot for her rounded frame. "Is this really where we want to be? I mean it's Christmas."

"Tonya, I love you girl, you know I always will. And when I settle, you can visit me anytime. That doesn't change the fact that I cannot give him a pass..."

I walked away as fast as my feet could carry me home. No, scratch that, to my dead relative's home. Nothing about this place was ever going to be home.

5
bearded gingerbread men

sebastian

I REACHED my hand into the ceremonial hat and stared DeWitt dead in her eyes. With her makeup done perfectly, her long sister locs curled and cascading around her shoulders, and her fluffy Santa hat set jauntily askew, she looked like a beautiful Christmas doll. Only I seem to understand that she was the possessed kind featured in every horror movie. All smiles for the public. Slash your Achilles tendon before stabbing you to death with a sharpened candy cane in private.

"You realize whatever I draw, I'm gonna kick your ass, right? The Bing family has won a significant number of holiday competitions. Even in the lean years."

"Pick and watch me destroy your little records like I always do."

With a smirk on my face, I pulled out a slip of paper that determined the starting contest and handed it to Mayor Garrett. Despite what Tonya warned, it was a bigger spectacle than I expected. Local media and the buzzing of what appeared to be the whole town, lit our little square with the kind of energy one would expect from a Vegas prize fight.

I showed my full set of teeth when the mayor announced the first competition of the season - holiday light decorations. I had it in the bag. I'd been planning out and setting up my yard just like dad used to. There was nothing DeWitt could do with my ten-month head start.

I stuck out my hand for a not so goodwill shake. "I'd say good luck, but there's really no point."

francesca

I couldn't let him sense on my worry. Rumor had it, the reason the Bings won the lights competition most years was because they spent the entire year planning.

Only an act of God could take those out.

And that's when I had a terrible idea. An entirely batshit, extraordinary idea... but first, I needed to get my team ready to go. After recruiting middle and high school students and some of my Grandma Mabel's friends, I laid out a plan for what we could do with just two days 'til judging. I needed to outwit Bing and create a fantastic wonderland.

Back at the house, I put on Christmas music, a big pot of coffee and brought out several of the sweets my grandmother taught me how to make. Cookies, sweet potato pie, pineapple upside down cake - all on her favorite serving plates. It was almost like she was here...

But she wasn't.

Looking around the house, still smelling her scent... I remembered the first time we met. I wasn't raised knowing my father's mother, and he never had good things to say about growing up in Ohio. Dad focused on building wealth and consolidating power. His position as a United Nations ambassador supported his ambitions, but it left me to grow up without a foundation of family support after my mother passed away. Learning Tonya and Sebastian were from Ohio Falls was a sign to me that it was time to meet what was left of my family.

Grandma Mabel was... warm. That's the only way I could describe her. She knew who I was immediately, and that first hug was everything good, wrapped in love and perfumed with White Diamonds. From that point on, every break and long weekend, I was here in this house or trailing after her around town like a found cat. I had a foundation to go home to like everyone else. Until Sebastian betrayed me. Those lost and lonely feelings couldn't do much for me, so instead I called Grandma Mabel's lawyer, again, and continued with preparations for guests.

I stood at a white board with schematics to the entire front yard. A large order was on its way from the local hardware store, and after much discussion, we had a theme and a plan. Everyone took their phone tree list for those identified as Team Frankie. We were gonna kick Sebastian's ass, but victory wasn't enough.

I had to crush him. Crush him like he crushed me all those years ago. Just the thought of his stupid, crestfallen face and lumpy, muscly arms hanging from broad shoulders in defeat gave me joy. And I took that joy to bed with me. Keep your dreams of sugar plum fairies. I dreamt of revenge.

And glittery, bearded gingerbread men with tight butts and low-slung scrubs. The gingerbread doctors wanted to tend to my injuries as they slowly cut off my clothes. Naked and spread open on the exam table, the head gingerbread doctor looked at me with lust in his little candy eyes.

"I may be the cookie, but I'm going to eat *you* up."

Oh, yes, doctor.

Soon the gingerbread doctors surrounded me and the one closest to my head stroked my face with one rough cookie hand while his other pulled at the waistband of his scrubs.

"Open. You're going to swallow all my icing."

Take my temperature doctor. I definitely need treatment.

The day of the Christmas lights judging arrived, and I woke with a hot face, wet panties, and an empty bed. Again.

It was ridiculous. My sex drive - hit and miss since I left my husband - had returned with a vengeance. My nights were filled with scandalous, holiday-meets-medical-drama themed dreams. Gingerbread men, Santas, even the eleven lords a leaping were having their naughty ways with me. Five golden cock rings?

Come on! No pun intended.

More troubling? All my nightly visitors resembled a certain stupid-faced man. Bearded, chocolate hued and in scrubs, they seemed to morph from their holiday items to a younger, then older version of the subpar veterinarian like a horny, shapeshifting Ghost of Christmas Past and Present.

I think I read that book once.

My phone rang, jolting me out of my thoughts. I hoped it was Grandma's lawyer, but Troy's name popped up again. I couldn't speculate why my ex-husband began calling me out of the blue. Everything had been said, signed and checks cashed. I blocked his number, tossed my phone into my open suitcase, pulled out my vibrator, and set Puddin' on the couch. Slamming the bedroom door, I flipped the switch, making a vow to beat Sebastian Bing today and find some strange peen tonight.

Later that Day Just After Sunset

Dressed in dark colors, I waited until a little after 5 p.m. Early winter darkness settled shroud-like over the town. Cautiously, I made my way through the backyard, over the small fence surrounding it, and through a couple of neighbor's yards. I was ecstatic to realize sabotaging Sebastian's display would be a lot easier than I imagined. Old home, a sagging power line, and a low-hanging branch for the win. The cosmos wanted me to crush Sebastian. It was fate.

After some quick digging around in the Bing garage, I found a ladder and a handsaw. I placed the ladder against the trunk of the tree and climbed carefully. I felt stronger, but not strong enough or young enough to scramble up a tree. Who was I kidding? I've never climbed a tree in my life.

Once I was there, I became one with the oak and shimmied onto the limb above the lowest one. Good thing too, the sagging branch looked rotted from my vantage point.

Looking past the limb to the ground below, I had a moment of pause.

I'm an adult woman with responsibilities and here I am in a tree. Am I really going to do this?

The original plan was to slip into their home, flip the master fuse, steal it, and slip out. I risked Sebastian and Tonya's dog Scout ratting me out, but the steak in my pocket would buy me enough time. Just as I was reconsidering, Sebastian came into view. Shirtless. Bearded. He was rubbing some kind of moisturizer all over his body. Over his chest, over the tattoo that decorated the spot running from his rib cage down into his black sweatpants.

Your stomach. Your stomach needs some too...

My telepathic horniness must have reached him because he diligently rubbed the concoction into his stomach. He was a solidly built man. Muscled about the chest, shoulders and arms, firm through the middle, just a touch of stomach area softness that made you want to hug him close.

He is a horrible human being, but the man is fine as hell. BUT he IS a horrible human being.

A text came in on my smart watch alerting me that the judging committee was closing in on the Bing home. Spurred to action, I leaned and ran the hand saw over the rotten part of the tree branch below. One swipe and it fell away with a loud crash. I didn't count on it being that easy and didn't consider the weight of the old, oak branch or the length. As it crashed to the ground, it sideswiped a piece of gutter, snapped the sagging electric line, and landed in front of, but thank God not on, Sebastian's truck parked in the driveway.

His house immediately went dark. I shimmied back to the ladder, climbed down, and shoved the hand saw into my coat. Creeping along the outer edge of the lawn in the dark, I felt eyes on me. Sebastian stared out the bathroom window at me, a single eyebrow raised, followed by a slow middle finger. It wasn't until I was a couple of houses away did he discover the full extent of the damage.

The absolute rage in his voice as he screamed my name made me giggle like nothing else. I hid for a moment behind a shed. Shirtless, he gave a quick search for me before moving to the front of the house - much to the delight of the judging committee, I'm sure. While he dealt with the committee, I cut through the yard next to Grandma Mabel's house. Quickly pulling on my hostess outfit, I listened to Sebastian rant live on the town's social media page.

"*She should be disqualified! She cut the branch! I watched her run through the yards.*"

"*I'm sorry, Dr. Bing, that end looks pretty rotted through. Luckily, there isn't any major damage...*"

"*This is some bull—*"

Out of breath, I sent the countdown text and took a quick look in the mirror. Waist snatched, booty right, locs giving what they should be giving. I looked *good*. With a few moments to spare, I flicked on my Christmas lights, hit start on the app and waited as houses all over Ohio Falls synched their music and lights to the beat. Every house that was Team Frankie, no matter their display, had a section of construction materials lit up with holiday figures appearing to be engaged in construction work. Every yard had a matching "Building A Better Ohio Falls" sign.

The lights blinked and twinkled all over town to Katy Tiz's "Whistle (While You Work It)"[1] and drone footage of the different houses was projected on my garage door.

We had converted my entire yard into a construction site

with various holiday characters hauling lumber, pipes, digging holes, etc. This late in the game, there wasn't much holiday decor left in the surrounding area, but the hodgepodge assortment worked with the "Under Construction" theme. The construction materials gave depth to the display. We covered everything in tinsel, lights, and a large "Building a Better Ohio Falls" sign stood off to the side, all aglow.

It was a humbling thing for me to witness so much accomplished with a simple little app and some good old Boy Scout and high school robotics club ingenuity.

When people come together, magical things happen.

I applied one more touch of my signature Rebel lip color, grabbed a plate of gingerbread cookies, and made my way outside just in time to welcome the judging committee.

"This is, this is really something wonderful," Mayor Garrett said as he considered my yard. He took in the drone footage on the garage door and shook his head in wonder.

"Well, this is what it's all about," I smiled for all the cameras live streaming, the mayor and the committee. "bringing the town together and working through anything that comes its way. There's Christmas magic here and if there is any place outside of the North Pole where you could find a better sense of Christmas spirit, you'd find a here in Ohio Falls."

The committee poured over the participating houses' map we provided and neighborhood kids ran to each house in search of stamps to collect for entry into the cookie raffle. Every neighbor came out of their homes and visited each other despite the rapidly dropping temperatures. The Christmas vibes were vibing and my heart was warm and full.

I felt him before I heard him.

"You witch."

"Dr. Bing, is that any way to react to *losing* a friendly competition?"

He slammed his hands on his hips. His camel-colored long coat contrasted nicely with his black sweats and hoodie. Not that I cared.

"Friendly? You just sent my house back to the 1700s. We don't have electricity."

I got nose to nose with him. Close enough to smell cinnamon and soap. Close enough to catch his left eye twitch ever so slightly. Close enough to where no one could hear me.

"This is Ohio Falls Sebastian. We both know not only do you not lock your doors, you don't have a single security camera in use. I'd like to see you prove I had anything to do with your unfortunate accident tonight."

His eye twitched even more. "You are absolutely insane, you know that, right? Who cuts off electricity to an entire house to win a contest?"

"An absolute winner, Sebastian, and I'm going to beat your ass like I always have. Then I am going to take those victories home and snuggle close to them every night."

"Your husband must be thrilled."

"I don't have a husband."

"Smart man."

Wow. That hurt. More than I expected.

The adrenaline rush I got from sparing with him dissipated and in my hustle to sabotage, I aggravated my side. The pain started to rear its head again. I slumped some and rubbed my side briefly. His eyes followed my movement.

"You shouldn't climb trees in your condition."

"I'm cleared to do whatever I want and I didn't climb

trees. I made cookies. Warm, delicious cookies that match my gingerbread men building a better community. Look around you. People are eating cookies and dancing. I won. Like a boss. And now I'm going to celebrate my victory at Ed's with a stiff martini and, if I'm lucky, a stiffer man."

Delighted to leave his mouth agape, I finished working the crowd until I was out of cookies. After congratulatory hugs to my team, I sent the kids home with pizza and invited the grownups to Ed's for adult beverages.

"Wait for me!" Tonya called, waddling over.

"Sis, there is no way you are going to the bar days within your due date."

"I'm not drinking, but I'm also not staying in a house with no electricity. Grab my bag out the car, I'm staying with Frankie."

"Ha! I won the contest AND your sister!"

"And I'm taking your bed for pulling that shit." She turned on me. "You owe me new gutters."

"HA!" Sebastian yelled as he dutifully got his sister's bag out of the car and hauled it, a giant body pillow, and a laundry basket full of snacks up my porch. He leaned in with a sinister growl on his way by, "I'm gonna get you for this DeWitt. I'm gonna bury you."

"Bring it. But first—JD! Hit my theme song!" A few swipes of the app and JD had the lights dancing to Jay-Z and Rihanna's "Run This Town."[2]

6
mr. right now

FRANCESCA

As I watched people mill about Ed's, I grew frustrated. [1]

"God, I could ride a face right now," I mumbled as I sipped my martini.

"FRANKIE!" Tonya laughed big, clutching her belly with one hand and her ginger ale with the other. "Keep it up and I will have this baby tonight!"

"Oh, no you don't. I don't deliver human babies." I took another sip as I surveyed the small bar full of couples, kids barely old enough to drink, and older folks who probably shouldn't mix alcohol with their medications. "I'm serious Tonya. It's been two long, dry mass battery use years. I'd pay $50 for a single man, under the age of sixty, with a beard to wet right now."

"A mustache would only cost you $25," a deep voice, full of amusement chimed in.

Barely recovering from her soul shaking laughs, Tonya introduced the sexy stranger. "Oh, you have done it now. Frankie meet Mateo Hernandez, the best ferrier in the county. Mateo, this is Dr. Francesca Johnson-DeWitt, the best large animal surgeon I've ever known. Outside the Bing family." Tonya's eyes lit up with mischief.

Oh yes. Yes, yes, yes, yes. Mr. Mateo had piercing hazel eyes, dark hair that hung longish around his collar, a wicked grin and, yes, a mustache. A most sit-able 'stache.

"It is a pleasure. May I buy you a drink?"

"I didn't say I was thirsty."

"Didn't you?"

Now it was my turn to smile. "Well, I guess I did in so many words. And you, Mr. Hernandez, are a tall drink of water. I could swallow you whole."

"Well, *shit*..." Tonya said fanning herself. "I'm headed to the bathroom. You two are getting *me* hot."

I flicked my eyes to track her exit and make sure she made it to the facilities safely before turning my attention back to Mateo.

"Now, where were we?"

"Flirting."

"Ah, Dogbreath DeWitt isn't the greatest at flirting," Sebastian said, interrupting and bringing in the cold air with him. He shook flakes off his camel coat and unbuttoned it as he plopped down on the stool beside her. "Destruction, yes, bossing around, sure, but the feminine art of flirting is as subtle as a cat in heat with her. Just ass up in the air."

I took my eyes off Mr. Right Now, and narrowed them onto Mr. Not Ever Again. "Beat it loser. The Ohio Falls Christmas Lights Queen is holding court, and I don't need a jester."

"You heard her, Mateo. No clowns allowed," Sebastian said with a toothy smile on his face.

"Am I missing something here?" Mateo asked. "Are you

two a thing?"

I gave the retch I seemed to reserve for Sebastian and turned fully to Mateo, crossing my legs and leaning in to give him more than a hint of cleavage.

"If we *were* a thing, it would be telling that I'm simply waiting for the socially acceptable allotment of time before sliding down *your* North Pole, Mateo. Suck Face here couldn't find a clit with a map and an 'Eat at Joe's' sign."

The grin dropped from Sebastian's face and his jaw hardened before he leaned back, tapping a cardboard coaster on the bar. "Like I said, as subtle as a sledgehammer. And believe me, Demure DeWitt, I remember *exactly* where yours is and the sound you make when I suck it."

My mouth hit the bar, his grin returned, and Mateo cleared his throat.

"And on that note, I'm going to leave y'all to...well, whatever this is," Mateo said with a tip of an invisible hat.

"Wait, don't listen to—" I started, but Mateo was already winding his way through the festive crowd. "Are you happy? That was Mr.—"

"Mr. Right? Oh please, Mateo is the biggest man-whore in the county. I just saved you from having your heart broken. Maybe slow down before jumping back into the dating pool, DeWitt. Things have changed since you were out here."

I signaled for another martini and moved from the bar to a recently vacated high top table. Sebastian followed. I growled and reminded myself that Ohio is a death penalty state.

"I deserve a medal for my good deed," he continued, oblivious to my glare as he sat and grinned even bigger.

"Please, you were cockblocking. Hard. And if I ever need

rescuing, *you* would be the last person I'd ask. If the choice is between an ax-wielding serial killer and asking you for help, I'd slow down so that muthafucka could catch up."

Sebastian barked out a loud laugh and took a long swig from the beer the waitress set in front of him. He slipped off his black beanie and rubbed a hand over his short hair, pressing down on his waves like brothas do. "I would do the very same, DeWitt. The absolute same."

"Whatever." I rolled my eyes, ignoring the amused look on his face, and scanned the crowd.

"Oh my God. You guys are in the same room and it hasn't devolved into a drinking competition? Or a darts contest, or arm wrestling? Are you both feeling okay?" Tonya mocked. She held her hand to my forehead in faux concern. Grabbing her hand, I licked her palm. She yelped, snatching it away as I cackled.

"Gross, Frankie, what is wrong with you? You've got a serious case of cute aggression. Always have."

I couldn't help but laugh as she wiped her hand on her brother's black hoodie in disgust and at the face he made. It was true. When we were all in school together, they knew me for loving cute things so much I wanted to bite and squish them close. Yeah, it's weird. Whatever.

"But at least I think you're cute," I reminded her.

A ringing cell phone captured Tonya's attention. As she stepped away, I signaled for my third and final martini. I needed to sleep tonight. Sitting in a house of memories real and wished for, in an empty bed, was more than I wanted to deal with. Plus, tomorrow I'd have to bake bright and early if I was going to win the pie contest. I was entering my absolute mouthwatering apple pie and Grandma Mabel's sweet potato pie. It wasn't enough to beat Sebastian. I needed to humiliate him in his favorite category and Grandma Mabel's sweet potato pie was so amazing that she stopped entering it in local contests so someone else could win. Grinning to myself, I wiggled in my seat.

"They make a cream for that, you know," Bing said over his beer, raising his eyebrows and looking down at my lap.

"Wait before you respond to that," Tonya said, holding up her hand in a calming motion toward me. "Sebbie and I need to get over to Mr. Richter's farm. Bengal has had labored breathing all day. Richter's worried he caught something from the circus."

"You're not talking about a tiger, are you?" My eyes whizzed from one sibling to the other.

"Bengal is a brown bear that Mr. Richter called himself rescuing from a circus somewhere in Idaho," Tonya explained as she rubbed her belly in wide circles. "We've been trying to convince him to send Bengal to a rescue center because he can't really afford to keep him and meet all the new exotic animal law requirements.

I nodded in understanding. There were a lot of exotic animal owners who had trouble meeting the new requirements - which was a good thing. If folks could be persuaded to give up their animals either through good sense or by law enforcement, they could prevent another disaster like Zanesville.

"I will never forget the terror of trying to keep up with the news on the ground after all those animals were released. Or the anger and sadness at seeing those endangered animals dead. We were on a flight to assist with capture and care when we learned we weren't needed. Broke my heart."

"Being here wasn't much better. The distance a scared lion or tiger can travel put Ohio Falls in the danger zone,"

Sebastian shared. He looked sternly at his sister and wagged his finger. "It's too late for you to go out there and it's more work than you should do this close to your due date. I can go alone."

"You cannot assess what I'm assuming is an adult brown bear alone." I pushed away my last untouched martini and put a hundred-dollar bill under the glass. "I'll go with you. Tonya, take my car home and take Puddin' here with you." I grabbed my Birkin off the dusty bar floor beside me and the puppy's head popped out with a lopsided grin above his inflatable collar.

"A seventy-thousand dollar purse and you have it on the floor," Tonya said, mystified.

"I'd care more about it if it hadn't been a 'Sorry I fucked my assistant, your assistant, and the billing clerk' gift."

Tonya's mouth dropped open.

I nodded and gave her a look that said everything without saying a word.

"Well, who did he sleep with for you to get that Hermès scarf?"

I reached inside the bag and tucked the scarf around Puddin' giving him a few soothing strokes. Shaking my head, I pushed down the embarrassment I felt every time I looked at that damn scarf.

"Oh that? That was a 'sorry I was fucking my assistant again and missed your dad's funeral' gift. I think the bigger insult is the scarf cost just ten percent of the bag. Or it could have been that the same assistant ordered and delivered the gift."

Tonya whistled long. "I would've burned it. And her."

"Nah, it's a tactile reminder - love is for the weak, stupid, and," I looked Sebastian square in the eyes, "the ditzy."

7
unleashed

sebastian

ON THE WAY back from our assessment of Bengal, I couldn't get what Francesca said about her ex out of my head. Nor could I forget the cozy scene I walked in on at the bar. Mateo eye fucking her and her encouraging it in that flirty little elf costume. The idea of her doing anything with him made my stomach turn. It would just be my luck she'd catch feelings and stay in Ohio Falls.

I glanced over at her as she tried to check her phone.

"There's no coverage out here. The mayor's working on it, but the actual work of connecting rural communities slows between federal elections, leaving local governments to push progress."

"Ah. It's kinda like infrastructure - everyone says it's important, but somehow it gets forgotten after the ballot box closes or until a bridge collapses," she said with a sigh, shaking her head. "I wanted to upload some videos of Bengal responding to my commands. He could kill me with one swipe, but will roll on the ground if I point and say 'bang.' That's hilarious. It's amazing he still trusts humans. Well, no matter." She put away her phone. "There's plenty here to keep me busy. I always forget how beautiful it is out here. There's something timeless about it."

I took in her profile as she gazed over the snow-covered stillness. Tall, dark trees, endless fields, and rolling hills that appeared to go on forever, made a living painting that I loved. "Why did you stop coming back?"[1]

She shifted uncomfortably in her seat. "I didn't have a choice, and no, I don't want to elaborate. Especially with you, of all people."

I ground my teeth to keep back a retort. The blood pulsed in my head as I remembered the years of work it took to recover from her revenge. The years my father worked to prevent bankruptcy... hundreds of thousands of dollars... my career delayed. I resisted the urge to slow down just enough to push her salty ass out of the truck. Instead, I adjusted the heat to give myself something to do. It worked for about four seconds.

Slamming my hand on the dash, I speared her with a look. "You know, out of the two of us, I got the worst of it. You act like the victim, but you made sure you left your mark on my life for *years* after what happened."

She turned to me, her eyes flashing and nose scrunched in indignation.

"I have no idea what you're talking about, but believe me, you cost me more than you could imagine. And for what?! I would have given you the notebook if you had just ASKED!"

"I DIDN'T STEAL YOUR STUPID NOTEBOOK DEWITT!"

"I DON'T BELIEVE Y — LOOK OUT!"

I snatched my eyes off her just in time to see a real black bear in the road. In my surprise, I over corrected. Between the ice and rapidly descending snowfall, we didn't stand a chance.

francesca

"Are you okay?"

"Yeah. You?"

"Yeah. Did you just Mom Arm me?" I peered at the arm stretched across me, then at the man attached to it. He was breathing just as heavy as I was. In unison, we turned toward the windshield. We were below the road in a deep ditch.

"We Mom Armed each other," he replied.

Looking down at his chest, I saw he was correct. "Yes, well, you can take your hand off my boob now."

"You first."

"Ugh! You're ridiculous." Snatching my arm away, I swept an assessing eye over him, scanning for any injuries. "You appear unharmed."

Sebastian did the same to me. "So do you."

"There are other ways to kill me and make it look like an accident, you know."

"There are other ways to feel on my chest. You just have to ask."

"I do not want to feel on your chest." I rolled my eyes at him and started to take off my seatbelt.

"Wait," he said, wrapping his hand around mine and the seatbelt buckle. "Let me get out first and make sure the truck won't slide more."

Staring at his hand on mine, I nodded.

I tried in vain to get a signal while also watching out for the bear in case it doubled back while Sebastian was out there. After a few moments, I heard shifting in the truck's bed, some scrapping and finally, Sebastian opened his door. He shoved in a canvas bag, some blankets, and other packages. He climbed in and quickly shut the door, but not before a blast of arctic wind smacked me in the face. I ducked down further into my coat, seeking shelter in a scarf I swiped from Grandma Mabel's closet. It smelled like her and made me feel closer to her, somehow. "What's the diagnosis?"

"We're stuck. We are going to need a tow out of here. And my main emergency kit is in my other truck."

I clucked my teeth. "Well, that seems irresponsible."

"Yes, it would be. Except the *only* reason I'm driving this old heap is because *someone* blocked my truck in with a gutter destroying branch to win a Christmas lights contest."

Oops. "Ok, let's not argue who's to blame—"

"You! You're to blame DeWitt! There's nothing to argue!"

"Ok, ok, sheesh! I'm," I gulped hard, "I apologize for my recent shenanigans and the resulting misfortune we find ourselves in."

"It's a fucking Christmas miracle," he scoffed, shaking his head at me. His chocolate eyes crinkled in mirth? Exasperation? I don't know what.

"You know what? I can walk. I don't need to do this with you." I opened the door, and that wind hit my ass, literally, and my soul shrieked. Scrambling to close the door, I let out a string of expletives that would put me on the naughty list for years. I flopped back into the seat and stared straight ahead, shivering.

A deep chuckle met my ears. "You done? We just need to wait for Tonya to realize we haven't come back yet so she can send someone out after us. Or for the road crew to come through. Until then we've got food, water, and blankets. And I've already lit flares."

"Okay Boy Scout, I see you. But if this is the backup emergency kit, what's in the main?"

"A satellite phone."

sebastian

"You're still cold."

I could tell she considered lying, but thought better of it.

"I am seriously regretting this outfit," she said, gesturing to the elf costume underneath her heavy coat. "Real pants would have been smarter."

She slid the coat up, revealing sexy tights with the garters attached. I instantly got hard. And irritated.

"When I opened the door, the wind went right up, well, you know. I'm supposed to be in the Bahamas celebrating my divorce with a stiff drink and a stiffer man. Instead..." She waved her hand at the world outside of the truck cab.

"I never said how sorry I am for your loss - the divorce and your grandma. Ms. Mabel was the best."

"I wouldn't know... not really. But from what I remember those two years I got to know her a bit, she was great."

I opened the door, and she grabbed my arm. "It's way too cold and snowy for you to be out there."

"I'm going to see how much snow I can shovel away from the exhaust and turn the truck on again." *Get my dick to calm down.*

"The snow is falling too fast, Sebastian. It's pointless. We are just going to have to use our body heat rather than risk carbon monoxide poisoning from exhaust backing up into the car."

And that's how I, Sebastian Bing, found myself snuggled tight against a dozing Francesca, recounting the grossest cases I'd ever come across. Just when I'd get myself under control, she'd shift or snuggle more into me, my body would react and I'd start talking about autopsies of pet squirrels with roundworms or infected cow teats. I must have drifted off because one minute she was telling me I was into the dark side and the next she was complaining about my elbow.

"It's really digging into my back. Wait that's not..." she muttered on a yawn as she shifted.

"I'm sorry," I muttered as embarrassment hit an all-time high. "I fell asleep and..."

She froze. "Oh, this is the worst."

"I said I'm sorry, just sit up and I'll—"

"You are not being fair. I'm hornier than a teenager with an underwear catalog, and you unleash the anaconda on me."

"I didn't unleash anything. I am very much leashed. Let's get that straight. And how was I supposed to know you're horny?"

"I'm fresh off a long, contested divorce, Sebastian."

She looked back at me like I should know something. I wasn't following.

"I was trying to pick up a man at a bar tonight."

I shrugged, "You called him Mr. Right."

"No, you interrupted me. *You* called him Mr. Right. I was going to call him Mr. Right Now." She mirrored his shrug. "You know, an easy piece of man to break the two-year streak."

God damn, two years?!

"Well, don't say it like that," she groused and turned back around in a huff.

"I didn't realize I said it out loud. But damn girl."

"This is the perfect scenario. Snow falling, alone in an old truck with a bench seat. Snuggling to keep warm...A hard... Well, anyway, it's not fair. I should be ass up, as you say, but fate has me here with you. You hate me."

"I do."

"And I hate you."

"Right... We could hate fuck."

8
hate you

francesca

HATE FUCK.

I rolled the novel concept around in my head, trying to rationalize my way through the idea of having sex with my nemesis. On one hand, it would keep us warm. On the other hand, it would let Sebastian Bing into my pants again. On someone else's hand, it would be an orgasm with another warm body for the first time in two years. *TWO. Years.*

I twiddled my thumbs underneath the blankets. "How would this work?"

"What do you mean? You just, you take all that anger and fire and fuck it out. You've never..."

"So, like make up sex..."

"Nah, this isn't reconciliation or reconnection. It's... domination. A release. There's nothing sweet or personal about it. It's... another way to fight."

He leaned forward, his lips by my ear. "DeWitt, sometimes I think about you and have gotten so pissed off, all I've wanted to do is press your face into the floor with that ass in the air and dick you down. Hard. Until you can't do anything but shut the fuck up and come all over me."[1]

He kneaded my thighs as he spoke, gripping them higher and tighter until he passed my stockings, moved underneath my garters, and grazed the sides of my satin panties. My legs, acting on their own accord, widened, giving him unencumbered access.

"I've wanted to fuck you until you begged for forgiveness, until you apologized, until you were soft, compliant and *quiet*," he growled low. "The more you talk shit, the more I want to wrap your locs around my hand and feed you my dick until your pretty lips swell and that throat of yours tires of swallowing. It's your fault the electricity's out DeWitt and all I want to do is bounce you on my dick 'til it's reconnected. It. Could. Take. Days."

He gripped my thighs even tighter, and when he swept one long finger over the top of my wet satin panties, I felt a jolt of electricity. I bucked slightly, and he sat back. I regretted the absence of his warmth at my back and between my legs. He was breathing heavy like he'd been running... and I was dripping. What the fuck was wrong with me?!

I wanted to hate fuck.

sebastian

I went too far, said too much, and probably scared the shit out of her. My heart pounded, clamoring to jump out of my chest. Now, not only did she think I was a liar and a thief, she thought I was a monster. A deviant...

I was so busy cursing my existence, I almost missed the moment she wrapped her small, strong hand around mine and slid it up her thigh. Slowly. Centimeter by centimeter.

I stopped her hand roughly and squeezed her thigh, tight, barely keeping a harness on the beast inside me. I took her loose hand and placed it on my iron hard dick. "We do this DeWitt, there are no soft feelings. No pretty words and no flowers in the morning. And when I beat your round ass in this Christmas War, you'll leave Ohio Falls and never come back, you hear? You'll get out of my hair and out of my system."

Francesca scooted forward in the seat away from me and disappointment and frustration filled me. Then she turned toward me on her knees and lifted her coat and elf dress higher, holding my eyes as she slid her matching green satin panties to the side. She moved to straddle me. Now, it was my turn to be apprehensive when she paused with her hand resting on my dick, over my pants.

"No one can know about this. And when *I* win this Christmas War, you'll finally come clean and tell the truth." She roughly yanked my sweats down and took me out. The sensation of her soft hands around me for the first time in years had me hard enough to break bricks. I grew harder still as she roughly jacked me, using my pre-cum to lubricate. "Then I'll leave Ohio Falls knowing I've bested you in every way possible. I *hate* you, Sebastian Bing," she panted, gripping my dick tighter. "I hate you so fucking much."

"Good. Show me."

francesca

"We do this DeWitt, there are no soft feelings. No pretty words and no flowers in the morning. And when I beat your round ass in this Christmas War, you'll leave Ohio Falls and never come back, you hear? You'll get out of my hair and out of my system."

His words hurt, and I didn't want to examine why. What I know is they were a spark, and I was parched, dry grass. He ignited a fire in me he couldn't contain. I wanted to hurt him; I wanted to feel good. I wanted that exquisite pain that leads to pleasure. I wanted to own him, to break him, and to break apart on him.

I scooted further up his lap and got myself in position. After lining him up with me, I wound my hand around the back of his head, my nails biting into his skull. He grunted and surged to join us. I lifted to deny him and give one last warning:

"It's been two years."

"I'll go slow."

Frustrated with his arrogance, I pushed his face to the side when he tried to kiss me. No pretty words? No intimate kisses either. I held his face away from me as I slowly sank onto him, relishing the pain and pleasure of spreading myself open on him. Of stretching myself to the limit.

When I was fully seated on his dick, I gave myself a moment to adjust, working through the moment by biting down on his neck. Hard. His grunt of pain turned into a moan of pleasure that made my clit throb. Moving my lips to his ear as I rocked on his dick, I grunted out, "It's been two years, Dr. Bing, and I'm going to wear. You. Out."

His hands found purchase on my ass, my teeth reconnected with his neck, and I leveraged the back of his head and the headrest as I moved my body with abandon. I threw my whole self into a sensual rhythm hell bent on extracting the pleasure I wanted, *needed*. I lanced open the wound I carried from his betrayal all those years ago and poured out that poison into each grind. I rode him hard and fast. I clenched and unclenched as I saw fit. I used him, used his dick for my pleasure, and came. Quickly. Beautifully. Fully.

Somewhere in the back of my pleasure crazed mind, I heard him say, "Slow down, beautiful. Wait, I'm gonna cum baby, not yet, let me give you..."

I fucked him harder, so hard the truck creaked metal on metal. So hard that there was no doubt I was running this, and he couldn't give me shit. As he swelled inside me, I ran wild, clamping down on his dick until he began to spasm. His hands dug painfully into my hips as he unloaded into me with a shout of surprise, bringing my second orgasm on.

It was now stifling hot in the truck. My body was slick with sweat and as the tremors of my orgasm left, my body relaxed. Panting, I let go of Sebastian's head and pulled back from his throat. His eyes were wide as he turned his head to me.

"Holy shit girl..." he panted as he swiped at beads of sweat on his brow. "Fuck. You get what you needed?"

I held his eyes as I unzipped the front of my costume and unsnapped the front snap of my bra. Rolling my painful erect nipples with my fingers, his dick pulsed beneath me. "Not even close."

His right hand left my ass and moved over my chest, stroking and plumping my breast as my body moved on its own again. He tugged at my nipple and I was electrified. Sebastian slipped a hand through the soft hairs at the top of my pussy and stroked me roughly. He slipped two fingers in and pressed his palm against my clit. Pumping in and out of me, he continued to press against my clit while stroking my spot. My moans filled the truck cab and his stupid, deep voice encouraged my orgasmic spiral.

"Take what you want baby, take what you need..."

I didn't want his encouragement. I wanted... I'm not sure what... My body was nothing but instinct, my emotions raw, fierce, and intense. Pressing my breast into his mouth, I commanded as I came, "Just shut the fuck up and fuck me."

Umm... Apparently, Sebastian had been holding back.

sebastian

The woman in front of me was different from the young, shy, sweetly soft Francesca I remembered. This woman was fierce, uninhibited, and aggressively self-assured in the value of taking her own pleasure.

She mounted me without hesitation, took without reservation, and that excited me like nothing before. I was content, pleased even, to let her take what she needed, craved, desired until it became clear she was dead set on destroying me with her pussy. The tight control I kept on the beast at the center of my sexual desires slipped a little with each rough bite she administered, and each rotation of her hips. When the minx wrenched an orgasm from me, I was helpless. My staying power has always been a point of pride. Even then, I kept the beast under my command.

"Just shut the fuck up and fuck me."

A voice I barely recognized growled, "Fine" as I gripped her by the throat to hold her in place and put *just enough* pressure to take her next orgasm, the one *I* was going to deliver, to the next level. My other arm wrapped like a vise around her, driving her down to meet me, pound for pound, thrust for thrust.

Grunts, moans, and the sound of wet skin on skin punctuated the silence that the late hour and blanket of snow provided. I took her breast into my mouth and bit the soft skin near her breastbone, relishing the gasp and the rhythmic clenching of her pussy. She was coming again, absolutely drenching me, and I extended my control, pulling out to her protests and maneuvering her into the position I'd dreamed of for so long. How we did anything in that truck, given my size, I'll never understand, but when pressed, a human can do miraculous things. Lift a car off a loved one. Run for miles beyond when the body wants to give out. Fuck the ever-loving shit out a woman you absolutely hate because she had the best pussy you've ever known.

I kept pressing her upper body into the seat and long stroked, deep and hard. And when she backed that plump little ass up on me; I fought through the urge to let her. The beast demanded I own her. I reclaimed her neck and pressed her further into the seat as I used my other hand to tip her pussy higher.

"You had your turn beautiful. You wanted me to fuck

you, I'm fucking you. Now be a good girl. Shut *the fuck up* and take. This. Dick."

A waterfall greeted my words as Francesca bit the blankets tangled around us and took my dick greedily, milking it for everything I had to give.

I gave her my disappointment. I gave her the hundreds of thousands of dollars the loss of scholarships cost me. I gave her the late nights working off bills from the lawsuit leveraged against my family. I gave her the pain of her throwing me away over a lie. And she took what I had to give. She took all of me and asked for more. She took me like she was made for me... and I hated her for it.

9
one to go

francesca

FAE... *Fae, wake up baby, uh DeWitt*... A sharp pinch at my nipple followed by a soothing, warm tongue brought me closer to consciousness. Leaning into the mouth at my breast, I moaned.[1]

"Shh... If you don't want Bill, our tow truck driver, to hear you come, I suggest you stay quiet."

That woke me. My eyes popped open in alarm as I frantically scanned around me. The sun crested the horizon and scraping noises rained down from somewhere on the road above us.

"You have until he gets set up to come. So... about two minutes."

"I'm not playing this game, mmm... Sebastian, stop. I said I don't want to be seen."

The hand between my legs stopped. The mouth at my breast paused and his hot breath drifted across my nipple.

"You sure about that?"

I hesitated.

"A minute forty," he whispered. "Thirty..."

It had been two years... and what was a fourth, fifth (?) orgasm among enemies?

"I hate you, Sebastian," I whispered in his ear as I rocked against him again. I ground down on his hand as he played with me. He was a virtuoso and I? His Stradivarius.

I wanted to stop, to fight him, but he made me feel so good. I chased my orgasm to peaks I'd never seen and a small part of me knew I'd never have this in anyone else's arms.

"I hate that this feels so good. I hate that... I hate ... God, I hate that I'm going to come again."

sebastian

The hot shower helped ease my sore muscles and the tension from my shoulders. As good as last night had been, and damn...it was fucking amazing, this morning was a cold reminder of the animosity at the heart of our activities.

After Bill's help with digging the truck out and towing it back to the road, the ride home went from awkward to fucking frigid. I closed my eyes against the memories, letting the heat and water pound against my back. It started with Bill finding Francesca's panties stuck to the back of my coat and went downhill from there.

"Well, there goes discretion," she muttered, looking out the window.

"I don't think Bill is going to say a word. He's not really the type to gossip."

"Men are the *worst* gossips." She took a deep breath in and let it out. "You know what, never mind, last night was a onetime thing. We've got it out of our system. I will beat your ass in this thing, finish Grandma's estate stuff, and be on the beach by Christmas Day."

I forced a laugh at her words. "Yep, all out of our system."

It wasn't out of my system.

"I heard you that day," she blurted as she stared out of the window. "I was late for labs. My dad and I argued about my Christmas plans. I wanted to come back to Ohio Falls. He wanted me to go with him and his latest wife to the Alps and said something off color about Grandma Mabel and the town. I told him about all the great things and people, including you. That's when he launched into a full-on tirade and forbade me to come back."

She shook her head at the memory.

"Anyway, I was late and upset, but couldn't wait to tell you I was coming back with you. I overheard you and some guys laughing. They were congratulating you on finally bagging me. I didn't mind that so much. Dudes always say stupid shit like that... but your roommate Swenson laughed and said you would have to have a golden dick to convince me to share my famous study binder. You said, 'This golden dick has already gotten me everything I'll ever need.' I didn't know what you meant until it dawned on me to look for my binder. I felt so used."

"I never took your binder, DeWitt. I was stupid, young, and showing off the fact that I, some regular brotha from Hicksville, had the baddest chick in school, not only as my friend but as my girl. I was immature, but I never stole from you. And the fact you still don't believe me..."

I eased my grip off the steering wheel before I broke the damn thing in half.

"Then what did you mean by 'This golden dick has already gotten me everything I'll ever need,'" she mimicked in the voice women used to make men sound dumb. "Why did they find my binder in your bag?"

I weighed telling her everything.

"Exactly," Francesca said, crossing her arms and turning further toward the window.

I pulled over in front of her grandmother's house as Tonya waved from the front door.

"I... I meant... I meant just that. I had everything. You had given me you Fae. You didn't just give me your body. I thought you gave me your heart and it meant everything to me...then. As far as I was concerned, I had it all. A full ride, a shot at a top internship, a plan to take over the family business, and an amazing woman with the world at her fingertips. Why would I give everything up for a dumb notebook?"

She stared at me for a long moment, still unsure.

"You disappeared," she narrowed her eyes at me. "You didn't even try to explain, and when I saw you weeks later, you had some tramp on your lap with your tongue down her throat. I pleaded for you to talk to me and all I got was 'Read the room Ditzy DeWitt.' I'd never been so embarrassed in my entire life. How could I mean anything to you if you treated me that way?"

"Fae, *you* disappeared. You just dipped. You didn't even come home for Christmas. You left all of us hangin'. Me, Tonya, your grandmother. By the time the semester started again, I was fighting for my life. I lost my scholarship because of your accusations. They said I violated the academic integrity code. I almost got kicked out of the program. They dropped me from consideration for the internship. My family was being sued and Tonya considered leaving school to help pay the legal fees. I hurt your feelings in a misunderstanding, and you torched my life in revenge. And with every victory after, you dance on the ashes."

The skepticism marring her sunlit face told me all I needed to know. She was still a spoiled brat, committed to being a victim. Nothing I said would change that, and I was done with the shit.

"You know what?" I said, reaching across her and pushing open the passenger side door. "You don't have to believe me. I made it anyway, despite everything you did to me, to my family. Tonya may want to still be cool with you, but I don't. Get the fuck out, DeWitt."

francesca

Tonya took one look at my face and rolled her eyes. She slow walked away from my grandmother's door and waved me in. Puddin' and Scout greeted me, dancing around my feet. I bent to give both pooches hugs and scratches, taking a moment to get some much-needed puppy comfort.

"I would ask about last night's adventure, but it's written all over your face. When do you leave?"

"What?"

"You. Leave. You and my brother had another blow up and you're going to leave us again."

"I —"

"Don't," she said as she threw up her hand with a sigh. "I'm just glad I got to see my friend again after all this time. Have a nice life, Frankie."

Tonya gathered her things.

"I didn't think you'd choose me over your brother."

"I didn't have to choose. He didn't do it. And you would have known that if you hadn't run off and taken the competitive streak the two of you have to unhealthy levels." She sighed a heavy sigh and shrugged in wonder. "You didn't take *my* calls Frankie... We were best fucking friends."

"He used me, and I was just so hurt."

"So was I. So was he. So was Mabel."

I shook my head. Dropping my coat on the arm of the couch, I sank deep into the cushion. "Grandma Mabel asked me to stay away. Given the choice between the golden boy of Ohio Falls and a granddaughter she barely knew, she chose Sebastian, declaring it was too awkward for me to come home... At first, she insisted it was until things cooled down. Then she found every excuse not to visit. Even for my graduation. I got the hint and let go. I spent that Christmas in hell with Dad, his work, his new wife, and new mistress. When I came back, I was determined to show everyone I wasn't the fool my dad said I was, the one Sebastian made me out to be."

Tonya sat next to me and placed her head on my shoulder. "I don't understand why Mabel told you to stay away. It wasn't like her. Whatever the reason, I know it hurt her to not have you here. She'd talk about you with such... pride and longing in her voice. And now it's too late to ask. Find some comfort in knowing she loved and trusted you enough to handle her affairs."

I shrugged, wiping away tears easier than I could settle the disquiet in my spirit. "I need to take a shower... and cancel my flight." Tonya's head popped up with a grin. "Too much is unsettled here, and my bestie is having a baby. No way I'm missing that."

She laughed as she hugged me tight, and I returned it as best I could with approximately eight pounds of baby between us.

"When are you due again?"

"New Year's, why?"

"The dogs won't let you out of their sight," I said, taking in the two pooches resting at her feet. "I hope you have your bag packed."

"I'm having a home birth, but everything's ready." She placed a protective hand over her belly with a relaxed grin. "I've been waiting for this little one for a long time. Here, help me off this couch before you head to the shower. Otherwise, I'll be stuck until you get back. I'll get out your baking gear."

"Oh, I don't think that matters anymore."

"Bullshit," she replied as I helped her to her feet. "The only way my brother will talk to you now is if you beat his pie. And you two *need* to talk. That truck boiled with anger, and you smell like sex. I bet you two spent the night hate fucking." She held up a hand when I tried to protest and pulled her long braids in a bun. "Hate sex is amazing. Amazingly stupid. Talk it out."

She waved a finger as she made her way to the guest bathroom. Two furry sentries - one big, one little - followed behind her. "Amazingly stupid girl. Heed my words."

Something gave me the feeling Tonya was speaking from experience.

sebastian

"Hey Frankie, can you help me at the kids' cookie decorating table?"

Fae hesitated. She looked around like she could tell I was waiting to sabotage her pie.

I was.

It didn't matter each pie had a randomized number to prevent what the Mayor called "more unfortunate incidents." I had a lady on the inside.

Tonya's glowing smile and tired walk made Francesca's mind for her.

"Of course, girl, who doesn't want to be covered in sprinkles and snot?"

"You still have a glowing appraisal of kids," my sister said with a laugh.

"I love the crotch goblins. I really do. I am also absolutely sure animals make less mess."

"Can't argue there."

Their lighthearted laughter trailed behind them as they strolled away to the activities tent.

I walked casually, weaving through the aisles of pies, cookies, and cakes until I spotted number twenty-three. It looked delicious. In fact, it looked suspiciously like Mabel's famous sweet potato pie recipe.

"That's messed up," I said out loud to no one. "She never plays fair. No one can beat Mabel's recipe."

I lingered until everyone was distracted by the children's choir and then made my move. A little creative decorating and DeWitt was out of the running. Satisfied, I whistled as I walked away. I was one step closer to being rid of Fae.

🐾🐾🐾🐾🐾

I almost forgot to look surprised when I heard Fae's screech from the back of the pie tent.

"Sebastian! You bast—ion of deceit," she trailed off as the crowd gasped and mothers covered their children's ears. "I'd like to file a protest. A formal reprimand. Sebastian Bing put fake cockroaches in my pie!"

In unison, the crowd moved away from her.

"Oh, come on people, they are fake. When have you ever see a roach this still?" She picked one up and waved it around.

"When it's been baked," I helpfully supplied.

"Mr. Mayor, this is an obvious setup. This one looks like it's doing the backstroke."

Mayor Garrett sighed. "Dr. Bing, did you put fake cockroaches on Dr. Johnson-DeWitt's pie?"

"No sir, I did not, and I resent the accusation, but I'm not surprised. Ditzy DeWitt is known for making false claims against the Bing family."

"Sebastian Joseph Bing. Rude!" his sister fussed from the other side of the tent.

Fae's face crumbled a moment before she quickly recovered. "I request the committee taste my pie and judge it alongside everyone else's."

"No way," Ms. Gladys said, clutching her pearls. Good old Gladys. I could always count on her to be a hater.

"I'm a vet. I would know if these were real roaches or not. They. Are. Fake." Fae pulled a second cockroach, the one I made look like it dove off the pie crust, and gave it a lick.

"Ugh!"

"That's so unsanitary."

"I'm going to be sick."

"Cool. Mom, can I eat a roach?"

The mayor was at his wit's end. "Drs. Please. Can we have one holiday activity where one of you doesn't do something that almost causes a riot?! It's supposed to be a fun holiday rivalry. This is Ohio Falls, not Sparta."

He drew his lanky length to his full height. "Now, Dr. Johnson-DeWitt, judging has concluded, and the winning pies selected. We cannot reopen judging to include a disqualified entry."

"But—"

The Mayor held up his hand. "I appreciate the competitive spirit and the town really appreciates your donation that allowed power to be restored to the home that lost service during the Christmas Light Contest," he gazed at her for a long moment, "but rules are rules."

In shock, my eyes moved from the mayor to Fae. She gave a simple nod and studiously avoided my gaze.

"She found a habitat for Bengal too," Tonya, now by his side, whispered. "Talk to her."

"I tried."

"Without your peen this time."

"In the hotly contested pie division, we have a tie," Mayor Garrett announced with a weary grin. Pie number thirteen, Dr. Sebastian Bing's 'Sweet Nothings' Sweet Potato Pie is our first winner.

The victory felt a bit hollow now as I walked to the small dias at the front of the tent. I kept my eyes connected with Fae's stoic ones. She raised an eyebrow, plucked another plastic roach out of the pie, and licked it. I was so taken aback I laughed out loud right there.

The mayor gave me a sidelong glance before returning to the information on his card. "The second first place winner is pie number ten, the 'Apple Bottoms' Apple Pie from ... Dr. Johnson-DeWitt."

"Whoo hoo! Gotta get up early in the morning to beat this DeWitt you twit!" Fae shouted as she power walked through the crowd and laughter rang out. She practically bounced onto the stage to accept her ribbon. As we stood for photos, she whispered, "Two down, one to go Bing."

"Dr. Bing, you've got a something on your collar," someone called out.

I glanced to my left and bug antennae greeted me. As I swiped at the fake bug, the photographers took the photo.

10
always time for pie

francesca

"FIVE MINUTES SEBASTIAN."

"You want five minutes to celebrate a tie?"

"No, I want five minutes to figure out the past."

That had his attention. I took a deep breath and set my pies on a table next to boxes and boxes of tissue paper flowers. We were behind the staging area for the parade floats, away from the prying eyes of the town. I'd had enough of people telling me they were "Team Frankie" or "Team Bing." And I didn't want to get into the bets. The white board with odds and all was now in the middle of the coffee shop on Main Street, for goodness sake. I watched Sebastian, really watched him, as I spoke.

"I never reported you to the academic council."

"What?" He looked genuinely surprised and confused.

"I never reported you. I only told one person what I suspected. In a rare display of parental concern, my dad called me back, worried I was still upset with him. I unloaded everything. I needed someone to talk to, and he was, for once, there for me. He tried to convince me to come to the Alps, but all I wanted was the kind of Christmas Grandma Mabel could give. The kind that restored your faith in people. Just a few hours later, she asked me not to come. She said things were too awkward with what was going on between you and me."

Our conversation was emotionally heavy, and physically overwhelming so I sat in the opening of Santa's sleigh on the nearest float and picked at invisible lint. "I thought you'd turned everyone against me or at a minimum, given a choice between you and me, Grandma Mabel and Ohio Falls chose you. I was used to that kind of thing. People not picking me. With Dad, it was his wives or side pieces. I thought you picked my notebook and clout over me. It made sense Grandma Mabel did the same and backed the hometown golden boy. Ohio Falls was the only place I felt unconditional love that settled in my soul. And I blamed you for losing that. Dad ranted and raved you'd made a fool of me, and I wanted to believe it. So, I vowed to best you in everything I could. To prove I wasn't a fool, or a ditz, or anything else."

Sebastian rubbed his hands over his face and considered me for a moment. He crossed the small space between us and sat next to me. "What about the lawsuit?"

"That's what I don't understand. What lawsuit? What did it have to do with school? And they were really going to kick you out over one incident? It seems extreme."

Sebastian looked at me in disbelief. "Fae, your father sued me for intellectual property theft, emotional suffering, and damages."

If he had told me he was doing alien autopsies, I would not have been more surprised. "For what?! For ME?! I never consented to anything. How did he even win a silly case like that?"

"He didn't have to. He just kept the lawyers busy for more than a year," he said, watching me closely. "The bills almost buried us. My dad kept working when he really wanted to retire. I finished that semester, stopped school for a year to work my ass off and pay for the lawyers. I needed to lift the burden off dad. I took out loans for the rest of school, so I didn't have buy-in for the clinic until a few years ago. You really didn't know?"

"God no! I was hurt, but I wasn't heartless, Sebastian. I would have never done that. How could you believe I would ever do something like that?" It made me sick, just heartsick learning all of this, and I couldn't stop the tears from flowing.

He just looked at me. *I thought the same about him.* Empathy is a bitch. If I was heartsick before, I was absolutely heartbroken now.

"Turns out my roommate Swenson lifted your notebook and later planted it on me. Tonya noticed he was damn near obsessed with that binder. So...she threatened to inject him with ketamine, then report him for stealing drugs."

So much to digest there.

"Ok, Tonya's hilarious and scary, but I don't... Yes, I took good notes and everything was cross-referenced, color coded and all, but it was the same information everyone else had access to. I don't understand why he cared so much."

"It wasn't the notebook, it was what it represented."

When I obviously didn't follow, he blew out a breath and shook his head.

"In Swenson's mind, there was no way we should be at the top of the class, ahead of him. He was convinced we were cheating. With your dad being a U.N. Ambassador, he believed your notebook was the proof, access to something like test questions or something. It really pissed him off to learn it was just a fantastic study binder. The Bings and Francesca Johnson-DeWitt were smarter than him *and* worked harder. *He* planted the binder on me after I told him what happened with us. I almost got kicked out for laying his ass out in the quad."

I could barely speak. I was full of sorrow and rage – and both threatened to cut off my oxygen.

"My dad contacted the academic council. He was the only one who knew." I sat with my head in my hands, warring with this new information and how it recolored my world. But the true victim in all of this was Sebastian.

"My God, Sebastian, I am so sorry for everything. *Everything*. I never meant for you, your family, to go through so much, and I don't blame you for hating me. I understand."

sebastian

The words I thought I needed to hear didn't matter anymore because she believed me. After all this time, what she thought of me still mattered. I thought I'd poured out everything eating me during our night together. Instead, learning the truth was the balm I needed for my... for my heart.[1]

"Fae, come here." I pulled her to me. "Shh...Fae, I don't

hate you. I never did. I hated that you left. I hated what you thought of me. I hated that it hurt for so long, but I never hated you." I tightened my hold on her. "Baby, none of that matters now," I whispered as I kissed her tear-streaked cheeks.

"No," she leaned out of my hug, "you were horribly wronged, Sebastian, and I had a part in that. I don't get to sit here and be comforted by you."

"The past stops being important when we decide to focus on what we do next. And right now, I want to hold you in my arms and treat you like the precious spirit you are."

I took her face in my hands. "You have been walking through this world, wounded and alone. Whatever I went through, at least I had my family and this town behind me every step of the way. You deserve that too Fae, let me. Let me be your strength."

She reached up, and with a cold fingertip, swept lightly over my brow. I reflexively closed my eyes and reveled in her touch. Tipping her head back, she offered her lips and I, magnet to my mate could not resist. And when our lips met I was home.

🐾🐾🐾🐾

We kissed long, and sweet as light snow fell around us. Slowly, sweet turned into more - passion and impulsive energy. No longer sharing tender kisses chastely on Santa's sleigh, it wasn't long before I had my Fae on her back unwrapping her as snowflakes kissed her face and settled into her hair. I grabbed a huge, thick, red velvet blanket likely there to keep a sweet Santa warm during the wholesome town parade and draped it over our nude bodies. With our coats as a bed, we tasted and caressed, re-familiarizing ourselves with bodies unencumbered by our heavy winter clothing. Bodies that had changed with time, but somehow still fit together perfectly.

"Is *this* hate fucking?" she panted as I entered her, slow and strong. Her eyes were intense and focused on my every breath.

"This is decidedly *not* hate fucking."

"Even though I beat your stupid pie?"

I chuckled deep, and I nibbled on her neck.

"It was a tie."

"Mine was better. You cheated."

This woman. I paused mid-stroke and pulled out. Fae whined and reached for me as I leaned part of my butt ass naked self out of the sleigh. Grabbing our sweet potato pies, I grinned down at her.

"I don't think this is the time for pie, Sebastian." She wiggled, trying to get me back inside her.

"It's Ohio Falls baby, there's always time for pie." Sweeping a thumb through the remainder of my confection, I held it to her lips. "Open for me."

She did the beast in me proud, opening like gates of heaven - legs and mouth. I rocked into her as I pressed my thumb into her mouth and she welcomed both, sucking my thumb and the sweet treat with a guttural groan.

"Fuck Fae, what are you doing to me girl?" Leaning in to kiss her, I tasted pie and her.

"Now that's a good fucking pie, right?"

"Yes baby," she said as she arched to me, "But mine is better."

"Show me."

When she hesitated, I fucked her into action. "Show. *Stroke. Stroke. Me.*"

"Oh, God!"

She reached to the side of me, grabbed a chunk of her pie, and rubbed it on her neck, across her breasts and down her stomach to the meeting of her thighs.

She was phenomenal.

"You are fucking phenomenal." Starved for her, I got to work tasting her pie. I licked and tasted her until she was writhing in agony and ecstasy. By the time I made my way to her pussy, I was ravenous and made a meal out of her pussy. Her taste, her scent. I couldn't get enough. I mean *damn*. I spread her open and held her in place as I lapped up everything she had to give me. I swirled my tongue to get every last drop, to caress and taste every single inch of her. Her undulating hips froze when I sucked her clit into my mouth.

Giving her my pie covered thumb, she sucked on it instead of crying out when her orgasm hit, and I felt that shit balls deep. After she rode the waves of her orgasm, I greedily continued enjoying my treat. Unconsciously, she scooted away.

"Where you goin' girl? I'm nowhere near through."

I held her in place as I kissed up her stomach, paying special attention to the dip in her waist that drew a sensual giggle from her.

Ticklish.

Filing that mental note, I turned my focus to her breasts and suckled at her neck. Gathering her in my arms, I held her to me so close and just... breathed her in. Surrounded by soft, luxurious comfort, I held her until I was sure she finally understood what it meant to be treasured. To be recognized as fragile and have someone invested in the care and keeping of her.

I held her like that through her next orgasm and my own. I held her that way after and she... She let me.

11
hit out

sebastian

A BANGING on the side of the sleigh made Fae squeak and squish closer to me, her beautiful doe eyes wide in surprise and humor.

"Alright you kids, you've got thirty seconds to come out from under there or I'm going to call your parents," Mayor Garrett called.

I kissed the tip of Fae's nose and tipped her face so I could taste those lips again. "Be right back."[1]

Making sure Fae was tucked in tight, I popped my head over the top of the sleigh.

"Mr. Mayor."

"Dr. Bing?" The Mayor looked around and lowered his voice. "Sebastian, now look, I don't care nothin' about how a man... enjoys himself in his private life, but there are kids and families out. And shit man, you can't be a single brotha out here butt ass naked in Santa's sleigh."

"He's not alone!" A muffled shout came from deep in the sleigh. "He's not alone."

Fae scrambled beside me, popping her own head over the top of the sleigh with the blanket held close to her.

"He's... Oof... He's not that kind of freak... Not to kink shame or anything," she added.

"Not that kind of freak?" I laughed at her insinuation. "Then what kind of freak am I, Fae?"

"Is that pie?" Mayor Garrett asked distractedly, staring at a wayward streak of sweet potato on the side of Fae's face. "Nah. Never mind, I do not want to know. I don't see a damn thing." He looked away as if he was admiring the other floats in the area. "All I know is that sleigh better be squeaky clean in time for tomorrow's parade."

"Of course, sir," Fae replied, holding in a smile.

"Mr. Mayor, can you hand me that apple pie?"

"Oh sure," the Mayor started toward the pie and stopped short when he realized what I wanted it for. "Wait, no! Go get freaky at home, Sebastian, DAMN."

Fae ducked back down in a fit of giggles. I shrugged and the mayor, to his credit, gave me a thumbs up before shaking his head and walking away.

francesca

"You look beautiful... happy."

I turned back to look at Grandma Mabel's door. Maybe I was hearing things or having a medical emergency.

"Troy. Tell me I'm having a stroke."

Not Stroke Troy chuckled. "I deserve that. I apologize for showing up unannounced."

"You should apologize for breathing. Why are you here?" I looked around the neighborhood, trying to both make sense of my ex-husband being there and to ensure there weren't any witnesses to his murder.

"I came to get my wife back."

"Am I smiling?"

Taken aback, Troy recovered quickly with a satisfied smile. "Beautifully."

"So, no lopsided presentation? Because I swear, I must be having a stroke. Or a nightmare."

I tried to walk around him and leave for the last contest - my fundraiser - but he grabbed my hands and attempted to kiss them both. Puddin's head popped out of his Birkin to growl at Troy. I snatched my hands back and wiped them on the back of my coat.

"I see you kept the bag."

He had the nerve to look smug and pleased.

"Yeah, the puppy takes a shit in it, and I use the Hermès as a piddle pad."

His smile dropped. Then he rallied. *Jesus be a board game and give this man a clue.*

"I don't know what's wrong with you, but we are divorced. For several good reasons, chief among them is your inability to keep it in your pants."

"That's all behind us. I'm committed more than ever Francesca. I've been thinking, since our divorce was finalized, I have a hole." He pointed to his chest. "Here. And only you can fill it. Baby girl, I've been watching your little games on social media. You're everywhere, on my phone, on the news...in my heart. I realized, I want to be where you are, anywhere you are, even here in this...little backwoods town."

"The ink may be still wet on the decree, because of you I might add, but I left you *two years ago*. There is no US, not now, not ever again. God, were you always this corny? Never mind, it doesn't matter. Go home."

I sidestepped him one last time and walked to my car.

"I'm going to prove it to you, Francesca. I'm going to show you just how committed I am and win you back. I know you hate me; I hate me. But I love you."

This was the man I pledged my forever. The man who should have been my home, but I felt no connection. Nothing but the passing familiarity of someone I used to know. "I thought I hated you. But the opposite of love is not hate, it's apathy. I look at you and feel nothing. Leave me alone. I mean it, Troy."

francesca

Pet hair covered me from head to toe, but we were finished. My teenage assistants looked decidedly worse for wear, as they were covered in hair *and* dyed in a kaleidoscope of colors.

"That's it y'all! The last pup beautified, last kitty blinged out and the occasional bird accessorized!"

Cheers went up around the large barn.

Tonya giggled from her seat in the corner as she sipped tea and rotated her hips on a giant blue ball. She said it was something about opening her cervix. All I knew was I not delivering her baby so she could open her cervix in this manger if she wanted to. One of our volunteers would have to catch it.

"We have raised almost fifteen thousand dollars," Tonya whooped. "Who knew giving doggie makeovers and kitty glow ups would raise so much?"

"Well, when you saw me turn Puddin' turned into panda, the squee you let out should have been proof."

"It's so cutely weird. I, like, have major cognitive dissonance. I know it's a pit, but he has a little panda face and I can't stand it! Tonya giggled as she made goo-goo eyes at Puddin'. Scout sat at her feet dignified in a black bowtie.

"Quick, everybody out!" Sebastian warned as he came running into the barn, his heavy peacoat flapping open.

"What's the matter?" I rushed to him, checking him over. "We've got a barn full of animals waiting for pickup."

Looking around, he grinned big. "Is that a Puddin' as a panda? It that a poodle with tiger stripes?!"

"Please focus. Is there an emergency or not?"

"Probably?"

"Sebbie, what did you do?" Tonya threw a tennis ball at him. The dogs went bananas.

"I thought we were good?" I yelled over the ruckus and looked in askance of him. He looked deeply apologetic.

"This was before the pie. As soon as you started advertising your fundraiser..." He rubbed a thumb along my cheek and looked me up and down, licking his lips. Heat rushed over me and I couldn't help but lean in and rub a hand along his dancing snowman sweatered chest.

"Sebbie!" Tonya reminded.

"Iputoutahitoutonyou."

"I'm sorry you, you what? **You put a hit out on me**?!"

"Not a lethal one. But there's a kid, Simeon, who's the —"

"The best or most notorious practical joker in town, depending on who you ask," Tonya chimed in. "Sebbie, that kid is an assassin!"

"Ok one, y'all have a town practical joker? And also, what. The hell. Sebastian!" I whacked him a couple times for emphasis.

"He's harmless, mostly, but he's a ghost. The kid has never been caught in the act. He puts them on his social media channels though, it's hilarious. I've been trying to call it off since I remembered this morning."

"Why are you just now remembering Seb!" Tonya looked around. "He could be anywhere…" she whispered, looking behind boxes of pooch dye and in the temporary kennels.

"I was distracted!," he gestured toward me. "You trying looking at this beautiful woman and thinking of anything else."

"Awww…" Six female and at least one male voice chimed in at that moment. *This place is sheer insanity.* I pinched the bridge of my nose to ward off a headache.

"Nice try Bing, flattery will get you nowhere. How old is he? Just call his parents… what's that smell?"

A few of the volunteers retched.

"It's happening," Tonya pulled her sweater over her face. "Peace bitches." She grabbed Puddin' in his Birkin, and with Scout following, waddled toward the door.

"I can fix this," Sebastian vowed.

"Fix it? What is it?" I wrapped my sweater around my face.

"Stink bombs. A Simeon specialty."

"Oh no, no, those are dangerous for the animals, the chemicals!" I ran around looking for smoke. "Where's the smoke?"

Sebastian sifted through hay and other things while the volunteers started putting animals on leads and in carriers to get them out of the barn.

"There's no smoke," Sebastian hoarsed out as he covered his face with his hand. "These are old school - actual rotten eggs."

sebastian

"I'll find the eggs. You get the animals." I looked for anything to keep the smell from burning a hole through my nose.

"Oh, you bet your cute ass you will."

Fae was furious. And she had every right to be... but... it was kinda funny.

"Are you laughing?!" she yelled from three kennels down.

"Come on Fae, you have to admit, this is a great prank."

Her eyes flashed, and her neck moved on a swivel. "Oh, it's great alright. It's great we are going to have to rewash everyone here who has this stench in their coat! We are supposed to be making money, not flying through supplies and man hours redoing a day's worth of work!"

"There are not many left. We can do it."

"We? We? Fuck you Bing. I'm not doing anything. YOU will rewash everyone who smells like the funk of forty thousand years. I'm going to get ready for the Holiday Sprinkle Dance. I will not spend another umpteen hours covered in animal hair!" She stalked toward the door and paused. "There are two eggs here."

Determined to mitigate the hilarious damage, I rushed over. I was focused on maneuvering the shovel to scoop the egg when a shove sent me into a vile mixture of rancid egg and hay on the barn floor.

The smell. Oh God, the smell.

I'll never eat eggs again. I'll never eat again.

It was worse than hoof puss or expressed anal glands. And I could feel it soaking into my clothes. I opened my mouth to yell at Fae and that was a mistake. The smell was a sulphur-like cloud that invaded my mouth. It was like the devil farted in my mouth. That sent me into the dry heaves. The more I heaved, the louder she laughed. She Beast.

God, I love her laugh. Also, Imma die.

"Yep, I'm gonna leave you to it. Pick me up at six. *AFTER* you bathe." She patted my butt with her foot and sashayed through the door.

sebastian

I adjusted the bouquet in my arms and sniffed myself one last time before I knocked. The rotten egg smell imprinted on my nose hairs, so I wasn't sure if the faint whiff I'd catch was me or phantom smells. It took only moments for her to yell out an invitation to come in.

I should have braced before I entered.

Fae looked ethereal in an ice blue gown that shimmered from every angle and enhanced every inch of her. Her locs, braided into a single braid and swept to the side, had tiny crystal snowflakes woven throughout its depths, making her look even more mythical. I wanted to be smooth, say something clever, but in the moment all I could do was tell her the truth.

"I missed you."

"Sebastian."

"Seeing you at the clinic made me realize what's been missing and seeing you now reminds me of what I never want to lose."

Careful of her makeup, I traced her cheek taking in the softness of her skin. Do you know why I call you Fae?"

She shook her head no.

"The first time I saw you we were doing field work. The sun had just begun to burn off the morning fog in the pasture. At first all I could see was a figure, and then a chill came over me. I can't explain it, but it was like the moment before magic happens. The split second when your senses sharpen and anticipation has you in its grip. And then... you appeared. You wore this thick Carhart jacket and heavy boots leading a herd of dairy cows. They were huge compared to you, but you had them under your spell. You looked like a working fairy and Fae, I got goosebumps, just like I have now."

"Stop, you're going to make me cry and I spent a long time on this makeup," she wailed as she hugged me. "You're supposed to come in and say something comically complimentary."

I took a deep breath to steady myself and to think.

"Comically complimentary? Ok... DAMN GIRL! You look like Elsa's melanated cousin at Howard's Homecoming, you frosty!"

She gave me a full belly laugh while striking a couple of popular social media poses. "That was so bad. You sound like some old school dude at the club."

"I am. Now, give me flowery compliments," I demanded, adjusting my jacket and smoothing out my beard.

She took my face into her hands, looked deep in my eyes and whispered, "You, who the gods chiseled from mahogany and obsidian, possess the beauty of legend. You are a king among champions, a man of valor, a pillar of grace. Prose of your magnificence will inspire a blueprint for heroes across all time."

"Fae."

"And you smell good, too. Cinnamon and soap. I saw you sniffing yourself as you were coming up the walk."

francesca

When we got to the Holiday Sprinkle, Sebastian went to work checking on everything for his run at the fundraiser contest. A brief kiss and he was off. I stepped further inside of City Hall's auditorium and ran straight into JD looking awfully smart in a chunky sweater, button down and dark jeans.

"Oooh weeee! Looking sharp there, JD! Hit me with a pose."

He obliged, and I whipped out my phone. "Now let's take a selfie!" Pressing our face together, we snapped a couple of smiling and silly pics.

"How could you let him look up to you and you're going to throw us out on our rear?"

Confused, I turned to find the source of the question - JD's mom and owner of the thriving coffee shop on Main. Clad in a sparkling red gown, she was as heated as the color.

"I'm sorry, ma'am, I do not know what you mean. I'm Francesca Johnson-DeWitt—"

"Yes, of Johnson-DeWitt & Thompson Inc. The same Johnson-DeWitt & Thompson Inc., that just dropped off a notice about a new landlord. Rent is going up by a thousand dollars next month. I can't afford that. This is Ohio Falls. Any progress we made over the last few weeks is gone, just like that!"

"Same here," Bill, the tow truck driver, clad in a smart three-piece suit, added. "Mine is going up sixteen hundred."

"Mine too," someone else called out.

"Don't you see what she's been doing this whole time?" Gladys asked gleefully, as she joined the growing circle. "She's been promoting Ohio Falls to increase the property values and her bottom line. But you all were too busy being 'Team Frankie' to notice something fishy."

"I've never heard of this company, and I didn't raise your rents. But I think I know who might have." I scanned the crowd, looking for my goddamn ex-husband. Instead, my eyes landed on Tonya in a beautiful eggplant empire waist dress that showed off her fabulous legs, cleavage, and high-top sneakered feet with Sebastian. He walked to me with determination. Something was wrong.

Oh no, not him too.

Tonya rushed after him as fast as she could, anxiety all over her face.

"Fae. Are you working to bring the Vet Co. conglomerate to Ohio Falls?"

12
grand gesture

francesca

"WHAT?"

"No misunderstandings between us, never again. You know this would effectively end our practice and Vet Co. would be terrible for the town. Their costs are higher than people can afford. They don't have large animal specialists and care more about pushing high dollar prescriptions and surgeries when there are better solutions that don't plump the bottom line."

I opened my mouth, but no sound came out. This was unreal and my anger had shifted to outright rage.

"Fae," Sebastian took my face into his. "Whatever is going on, I love you. I have your back and we can work together to figure this out. Tell me what's going on and I'll believe you."

The vise around my heart eased and I got lightheaded, but I nodded anyway. "I didn't do this," I whispered. "I can't believe this is happening again." I looked up into his face and saw sweetness. I saw support. I saw love. Sebastian traced his thumb across my cheek, tipping my chin up for a kiss.

"I believe you."[1]

His mouth found mine and I was lost. Relief, gratitude, and something bigger flooded me. Sebastian touched his forehead to mine. "We'll figure this out."

"My ex, he's created some bogus company. I never signed anything." Panic creeped into my voice. "He's here talking about getting back together."

"Well, he's too late, you're mine."

"I am? Shouldn't we discuss this?"

"These folks' whole lives are collapsing. You really want to have the boyfriend/girlfriend discussion now?"

"We are a little old for those titles."

"Fae baby," he booped me on the nose. "Focus."

Turning to the crowd, Sebastian got their attention. "Folks, there has obviously been some misunderstanding. I can guarantee, on my name, that we will figure this out. Until then, let's just enjoy the Holiday Sprinkle."

With some reluctance, the crowd dispersed but not before the mood of the event soured. Poor Mayor Garrett... It was a cold reception when he announced Sebastian's fundraiser. People who worry about their livelihoods won't spend money they aren't sure they have, no matter the cause.

"I'm so sorry Sebastian. All of this is sinking your auction." Item after item went up and sold for next to nothing. The crowd lost its energy even as Mayor Garrett did his best to get them going again.

"You'd do anything to win huh?"

I scoffed. "Not even I would have thought of this."

He looked at me with a gorgeous, determined smile. "We'll figure it out Fae. There's always a way. Trust me."

Leaning into him I gave him my weight, secure in knowing he'd support me. "I do. With everything in me."

He gave me a look of such tenderness; the world fell away. Kissing me again he held me close and whispered in my ear, "Remember that in about thirty seconds."

🐾🐾🐾🐾🐾

"Now for our last item, I know you're going to go crazy for this. Maybe that's why everyone's being so tight with their cash. Win one outing - lady's choice - with a hometown hero. A person who has worked, to astounding success, suspicious events and pranks notwithstanding, to put our town of Ohio Falls on the map..."

I turned and looked up at Sebastian. He was putting himself up to raise money for families affected by the closing of the shipping distribution centers! He'd have to learn I wasn't the jealous type, especially for something like this. I looked around for my paddle to help drive up the price.

"Dr. Francesca Johnson-DeWitt!!"

The spotlight swung around to me just as my eyes narrowed on Sebastian. "You signed me up to win *your* fundraiser?"

"It's a brilliant idea actually."

"Yeah well, jokes on you. I'm now the town pariah."

"Even I couldn't have predicted that rapid turnaround She Beast," he joked, booping me on the nose again. "It'll be ok my beautiful Fae. I promise."

"Come on up Frankie!"

I climbed the stage steps to a smattering of anemic applause.

Tough crowd.

"Let's start the bidding at fifty dollars."

Silence.

"This is for an outing with the famous leader of Teeeaaaam Frankie," the Mayor tried again.

Crickets.

There are times in a human's life that are destined to be three-a.m.-keep-you-from-sleeping moments. This was one of them. It. Was. Painful.

I reached out for the mic, and our confused mayor passed it over with a shrug.

"The rumors are not true. I have nothing to do with the notices you are receiving. I haven't purchased any real estate in Ohio Falls. Anything with me listed as an owner must be a fabrication because I have never signed a single piece of paperwork, napkin, or scrap of toilet tissue for a company named Johnson-DeWitt & Thompson. I'm here solely as Mabel Johnson's granddaughter fulfilling her final wishes. By the way, if you see a Mr. Maxwell Burnside, tell him I'm looking for him. Now, can I get a little trust and fifty-five dollars for a great cause?"

"Sixty."

"Seventy."

"One hundred dollars."

"One fifty."

sebastian

She's amazing.

I watched as she turned the entire auction around. Sure, he'd lose this battle and the overall war, but he didn't want to win. He wanted Fae to choose to stay in Ohio Falls. So yes, he was perfectly happy to lose to Dr. Francesca Johnson-DeWitt one more time.

"FIFTEEN THOUSAND DOLLARS."

Red covered my vision as a slick muthafucka in a gaudy black and gold tux carried a gigantic bouquet of roses through the crowd.

A second spotlight highlighted the jerk as he stood below the stage grinning a too white, too perfect smile up at my Fae.

"Fifteen thousand going once," the mayor reminded.

A collective gasp flitted through the crowd as the asshole, whose body would never be found, got down on one knee.

"Francesca, will you marry me. Again?"

"Fifteen thousand going twice..."

"TWENTY THOUSAND DOLLARS."

"About time," my sister grumped from my side.

I strode to the stage.

"I'm sorry Sebastian, you can't bid in your own auction."

"Dominic, you don't want to get on my bad side."

"Rules are rules."

"You are not going to turn down twenty thousand dollars."

The mayor seemed to be considering my point when Fae proclaimed with effortless calm, "Fifty thousand dollars." She stepped closer to the front of the stage and eyed both of us from her strategically advantageous location. "I can take care of myself. Troy, if I had to choose between an ax-wielding serial killer and marrying you again...

"...I'd slow down so that muthafucka could catch up."

"She'd slow down so that muthafucka could catch up."

We spoke at the same time and fell out laughing.

"Uh, I believe we have fifty thousand dollars going once, going twice..."

"FIFTY THOUSAND AND ONE DOLLAR."

Tonya made her way next to me smiling. "JD and I know you can take care of yourself, but you don't have to. Not in Ohio Falls. Not while we're around."

francesca

The agreements and cheering from the crowd swelled and threatened to drown my heart in overwhelming goodwill. Blowing a kiss out to everyone I quickly descended the stairs and hugged my bestie, tight. Throwing my arm around JD I brought him into the love fest as well.

"Hey Frankie, sooo... I need to borrow forty nine thousand dollars," Tonya said with a mischievous grin.

"Ha! I had a feeling. What's mine is yours girl. Always."

"This is my grand gesture, Francesca," Troy pouted waving the roses. "I bought you this raggedy little town you love. What more do you want?"

I loosened my hold on Tonya and JD and looked Troy in the eye for what I hoped would be the last time.

"Nothing Troy. I want absolutely nothing from you." Sinking into Sebastian's arms I tried to walk away.

"I bought a whole town for you. I'm killing his practice and suing him," he said pointing at Sebastian, "for you!"

"Dr. Sebastian Bing?"

"Yes?"

"You've been served."

I watched the very familiar process server walk away.

"Did you... Did you bring your assistant, the same assistant you cheated on me with, to 'win your wife back?'"

"Well," he shrugged, "she's a good assistant."

My entire life crystalized into acute understanding. "OH MY GOD. YOU ARE JUST LIKE MY FATHER! I married my *fucking* father." I shook my head in amazement. "Talk about daddy issues. You check all *his* boxes. Using money to bully and intimidate. The lies and tricks. The rotating stable of women... Jesus! And if you know his tricks, you knew what he did to the Bing family!"

I was screaming at him I was so livid. At myself. At Troy and my father.

"He warned me about this town, about keeping you away from here. He didn't want you to throw your life away for a holiday movie cliché like his mother. At least he had good enough sense to make sure she kept her distance," Troy stood tall, malice in his eyes. "End this tantrum or I raze this place to the ground. Come home."

I could feel Sebastian's dangerous energy reach critical. His fists, balled into knots in his pockets, were vibrating against me. I held a soothing a hand to his chest and squared up with Troy.

"Let me guess, the official looking documents you toilet papered the town with haven't been filed with the appropriate agencies. Yet. You're going to use panic and confusion to play one side against the other, bury people in paperwork then swoop in with cash to make it all go away. Or do you plan to buy the mayor and other officials to eminent domain your way? You can't pull that here, this community believes in each other and they can't be bought or fooled."

Troy looked around, uncomfortable at being exposed. "You belong with me, Francesca. I want you, only you."

"MY HEART DOESN'T RELAX, TROY. I'm on two medications because of my blood pressure and that's on you. You nuked our marriage vows and dragged our divorce out for two years to manipulate me. You literally broke my heart and it's STILL NOT ENOUGH FOR YOU."

I shook my head in wonder. "I've had enough pie to wash your poison out of my system. I told you, I feel nothing for you, but know this: you fuck with this man right here or this town and *you* won't be the villain of this story I will. You don't have the imagination to dream of the nightmare I will become. Starting with the forgeries of my signature, sliding into the intimidation tactics to scare people out of their businesses, skipping right to the double books your businesses keep, your offshore accounts, the insider trading and off the books campaign donations."

I got thisclose to him and yanked him by his bowtie so I could whisper in his ear. "And while I know several ways to kill a man and make it look like a legitimate medical emergency, I want you to live. Live to see what I will do to the rest of your family. My father warned you about this town. He should have warned you about me. There is not a secret your family has that I haven't known since the day I *married* you. You can thank my daddy for that. You have lived under grace you were unworthy to receive. So, try me, Troy. You'll find I can be moved from disinterest to ardent passion with the proper motivation."

Letting him go, I fixed his tie, brushed a few errant pieces of lint off his shoulders and gave him a pat.

"Are we going to have a problem Troy?"

He grit his teeth and venom lived in his eyes.

"No."

"Are the people of Ohio Falls going to have a problem, Troy?"

"It would've been legal if—"

I held up a finger. "Titus."

Troy's eyes grew as wide as saucers. Visibly gulping, Troy found his voice. "They will not have any problems."

Giving him one last look of dismissal, I turned toward the stage. "Mr. Mayor, tell the DJ to play my Sebastian's song. He won, so he gets first song choice, right?"

Grinning, Mayor Garrett nodded. "Sebastian requested this special for the amazing Dr. Francesca Johnson-DeWitt. He said and I quote, 'This was worth the wait.'"

He signaled the DJ and Sebastian grabbed me close and kissed my forehead, nose, and lips. I wrapped my arms around him, snuggling as close as I could, preparing for a love song.

No one laughed harder than I did when Ludacris' "Move Bitch" [2] boomed over the speakers.

Grinning at him as we slow danced to one of the rowdiest songs I've ever had dedicated to me, I caressed his cheek with my thumb like he's done so often with me. "I love you Dr. Sebastian Bing. Even more than I love winning."

His smile lit like the star of wonder and he gripped me tighter.

"Good, because you'll never beat me again."

"Uh, I believe we are tied, and you only won tonight because of me."

His soulful, dark eyes widened at my audacity. "I almost lost tonight because of you too!"

"No, that was Troy's dumb ass. Forged signatures," I shook my head.

"What did you say to him and what's 'Titus?'"

"I took a page out of Tonya's book with a lil' sprinkle, sprinkle of my own. Troy has a spending problem and soon, an IRS problem. Titus is not as mysterious as it sounds. His father, who likens himself a gangster, has a boat -Titus- where he conducts 'special business.' Troy thinks it's hardcore mobster stuff, tossing bodies. It's his parent's monthly swinger excursion. I let Troy think I knew where the bodies were. There are bodies, just consenting, horny septuagenarians."

We laughed in each other's arms and wiped away tears of mirth from both of our faces.

"Excuse me, Dr. Johnson-Dewitt?"

We paused in our laughter long enough to greet an older gentleman who looked nervous as hell.

"How can I help you?"

"I'm Maxwell Burnside and I'm afraid I have terrible news."

13
you have me

sebastian

I WAS on high alert as I ushered Fae and Mr. Burnside to an empty room off the auditorium where it was private and quiet. Tonya and I made eye contact and spoke without saying a word, like we've done all our lives. She grabbed the Birkin and joined us, placing her hand on top of mine at the small of Fae's back.

"Do you want us to stay, Fae, or do you want privacy?"

"After the day I've had, I need you. Both of you. Stay and help me, please."

"You have me, baby. You have us."

We led Fae to one of the conference room chairs. Tonya and I sat on either side, each of us taking one of her hands.

"I'm just going to come right out and say it," Burnside started, wringing his hands as he paced. "Nothing like this has ever happened. I have always followed the letter of the law to a 'T', and I promise you, I will make restitution."

"Not to be rude, Mr. Burnside, but I'm about to lose it

here. Please, just tell me what's happened," Fae said, squeezing my hand and bracing.

"I've been avoiding you as I tried to remedy the situation, but... I lost part of your inheritance from your grandmother Mabel DeWitt's estate. She trusted me. We were special friends until the Lord took her far too soon. She was a beautiful woman inside and out and I... I would have done anything for her. I am so sorry I could not do this last thing."

Tonya and I shared another look, then she raised a brow. She thought the same thing I did—Burnside and Mabel had a thang. And while he had my sympathies, he also had my ire if he'd taken advantage of Mabel and Fae.

"Get to it Burnside," Tonya snapped as she adjusted in her seat and took in a deep breath.

He hung his head. "I lost your puppy, Franklin."

Collectively, our heads tilted in dog.

"I'm afraid I don't understand. Grandma Mabel left me her dog?"

"She bought him for you. She thought her granddaughter would need a loyal friend after your father died and the divorce. She was waiting for him to be ready to leave the litter and be trained so he would be a good a companion. She passed before she could bring him to you. I kept him at my home while I waited for your arrival, but he got out the day they delivered her ashes. I was...Not myself and he must have slipped right out. I've been looking for him for days, calling every dog rescue and warden in the area and beyond. I've combed the streets, but Franklin is a purebred Staffordshire Bull Terrier, quite valuable, and I think another family or someone who knows his value has scooped him up. Please accept my sincerest apologies. I know another pet can't replace one handpicked by Mabel, but I'd like to try."

"Do you mean this Staffordshire Bull Terrier?" Tonya reached into the Birkin and pulled out a sleeping Puddin'.

"Oh, my goodness, Franklin!"

The puppy we knew as Puddin' wearily opened one eye and yawned. Stretching, he looked around until he spotted Burnside, then his tail went crazy. He took off across the conference table and gave happy yips and full-face licks to the overcome lawyer.

After a moment, Burnside gathered himself and gave Franklin the command to sit, to which the pup happily obeyed. Burnside gave him a treat.

"I kept them in my pocket in case I found him," he explained sheepishly. "Where did you find him?"

"He was on Grandma's back porch when I arrived. I spooked him and we got into a minor scrape, but we've been buddies ever since." Fae sighed happily. "And he's been a good guard pup for Tonya while she's on baby alert."

On cue, 'Franklin' trotted back over to Tonya and nose bumped her baby belly before settling back on the table.

"Why didn't you contact us, Mr. Burnside?"

"I did Sebastian. Your front desk associate said no one turned in a dog like Franklin and they would call if he showed up."

"That makes sense," Fae said, smiling, with tears in her eyes. "We arrived well after closing and the clinic wasn't open the Sunday I picked him up. She really did love me."

Heart full, I wiped the tears from her face. She deserved this.

"Oh, she thought you hung the moon Francesca," Burnside confirmed with a gentle smile. "She hung onto hope she'd make it back into your life, but time just wasn't on her side. There is a special place in hell for what your father did, keeping you two from each other, especially after you met, but he was a proud, angry, unforgiving man. He hated his common roots and hated that his mother embraced them. He thought it made him look weak, and he didn't want you 'settling' for small town life with a poor church mouse lawyer." Burnside's eyes flamed, and he took a moment to collect himself again.

"He threatened to cut *you* off if she didn't keep you away and later, threatened to close your practice if she reached out. She saw what he was doing to the Bings, saw how difficult it was for Sebastian to continue his education and, as painful as it was, she chose you Francesca. She broke connection with her only granddaughter so you could have the life you wanted and soar to heights beyond what she could give you with her modest life here. On two conditions—your father had to keep her in the loop on everything going on in your life and he had to drop the lawsuit against the Bings."

Tonya, Burnside, and I sat with Fae while she processed. My heart was torn to pieces for her and Mabel and what they'd lost. I also felt intense gratitude Fae got this last opportunity to know her grandmother's heart. And that Mabel used her last bargaining chip to protect *my* family. If I could take this pain from her I would do it without hesitation, but I had to be content to hold Fae until the tears slowed. Tonya rubbed her back and Franklin "Puddin'" Johnson-DeWitt sat with his head on her hand, giving her the occasional encouraging lick.

"Thank you, Mr. Burnside. Thank you for giving me this and thank you for loving my grandmother."

Burnside gave a small, sad smile. "At the risk of being unprofessional, I could breathe because she moved in this world. I will cherish the moments I had to love her... forever." After using his handkerchief to wipe away the wet, he straightened himself up.

"One last thing Francesca and I'm going to let you young people go dance the night away, or at least until eleven thirty, when this shindig ends. You have a considerable property inheritance alongside a small monetary fund. Your father, likely in his guilt or as hush money, tried to make sure your grandmother was *comfortable* after forcing the break in your relationship. He didn't know his mother, or he forgot there were still people with morals. Regardless, your grandmother invested every dime in real estate around Ohio Falls. Mostly commercial. It's not as lucrative as it could be with the shifts in industry happening, but there are some offers on the table for the properties, including a new party who seems very interested. I have not vetted them. My search for Franklin consumed my every moment, the scamp. He shuffled some papers around. "Ah yes," he paused, confused. "Johnson-DeWitt & Thompson Inc.?"

"This mutha—"

"Win me back my a—"

"No way he's that smart."

We all spoke at once, with Fae giving Burnside a quick rundown of everything.

"And he could be that smart Sebastian. He's just too self-absorbed to put forth any genuine effort. His assistant, however, is superb."

francesca

It had been one helluva night. The stuff of legends and nightmares. But as Sebastian and I walked arm in arm through the quiet, snow-covered gardens behind City Hall, I focused on what mattered.[1]

For a moment, I had my grandmother back. Secretly, I had hoped for a letter or video from beyond the grave explaining why she pushed me away all those years ago, but life does as it does. Sometimes, people simply run out of time to say the things they want to say. It was a bittersweet pill because, while I didn't have one last letter; I had the reason. I had confirmation of her love for me, and I had Grandpa Burnside. That's what he asked me to call him.

He and grandma were "special friends" for over thirty years. They met playing cards. After her first husband died, she joined a Bid Whist club to cope with her grief and loneliness. They never married because Grandma Mabel, and I quote, "was done with being someone's wife." Grandpa Burnside didn't care, he only wanted Mabel, however he could be with her. He promised me, if I wanted, he would stand in for Grandma, share all his memories of her and love me like she did.

I wanted.

I shivered against the cold despite my coat and Sebastian's warm body.

"Are you ready to go home, my Fae?"

"Yes. I baked."

Sebastian's eyes grew lazy with lust, and he pulled me to him, pressing his erection into me. "Apple? Sweet potato?"

"Gingerbread."

"Gingerbread?"

"You'll see."

As we stopped in City Hall to collect my purse and Puddin', we crossed paths with Tonya and Mayor Garrett as they came back from the nacho bar.

"So," Tonya asked, "how are you two going to break the tie?"

"Well," we looked at each other and shrugged, "there's always Kwanzaa."

A bear and a mayor walk into a bar...
Want more Sebastian + Fae high jinks? Check out the epilogue to The Christmas War Paws here:
https://BookHip.com/GJRLVSK

Want to talk books?
Join my Facebook group:
Terreece's Thirst Trap (bit.ly/terreecethirsttrap)

also by terreece m clarke

Contemporary Romance

Heartbeat
The epic love story of Mike and Maya that started it all.

Love Never
The 96 hour love story of Elise and Smooth - Maya's parents.

Chaser
The love story of Shay and Xavier.

Fingertips
The love story of Selene and Fox.

Breath
The love story of Juliette and Logan (Wolf).

The Christmas War Paws
A hilarious enemies to lovers novella

Adult Coloring Books
Black Girl Magic Mandala
Book Boyfriend Adult Coloring Book

about the author

Bestselling author and journalist Terreece M. Clarke writes epic love stories about smart, courageous Black women loved without reservation or hesitation.

A longtime journalist, she has written for various websites, magazines, newspapers, and as a YA and children's book reviewer for Common Sense Media. Her work has garnered the attention of the New York Times, Disney, and Jezebel, and her company's digital marketing clients have landed media appearances for national outlets including Fox Business News, BET, CNN, Ebony Magazine, The Root, and MSNBC.

As a successful writer, journalist, entrepreneur, mother of three, and wife to one, she is often asked to lead discussions on women and parenting issues and diversity in media, pop culture, and tech.

Terreece's first book - "Olivia's Potty Adventures" a potty training storybook featuring an African American character - spent 16 weeks as a top new release.

Heartbeat: A Courageous Love Novel, her debut romantic suspense novel became a top international romance novel in two categories.

You can find Terreece writing through life on TikTok, Instagram, and Facebook - come join the conversation!

- tiktok.com/@terreece
- amazon.com/Terreece-M-Clarke/e/B07746K4WN
- bookbub.com/authors/terreece-m-clarke
- goodreads.com/terreececlarke
- facebook.com/terreecemclarke
- instagram.com/terreece
- x.com/terreece

www.ingramcontent.com/pod-product-compliance
Lightning Source LLC
LaVergne TN
LVHW030323070526
838199LV00069B/6544